DEADMISTRESS

A Susan Lombardi Mystery

BY

CAROLE B. SHMURAK

\

ISBN-13: 978-1456324186
ISBN-10: 1456324187

First Printing: 2004 SterlingHouse, Pittsburgh PA
Second Printing: 2007 SterlingHouse, Pittsburgh PA
Third Printing: 2011 Park Court Press, Farmington CT

NOTE TO THE READER:

There has been no town called Wintonbury in the state of Connecticut since 1835. Neither Wintonbury Academy for Girls nor Metropolitan University exists. The administrators and faculty of these institutions are also figments of my imagination. But there are many girls like Nini and Shauna; I know because I taught them.

For reasons that will become apparent later in the book, all of the quotations used as epigraphs may be found in *Bartlett's Familiar Quotations*.

ACKNOWLEDGMENTS

I would like to thank the friends who read and made suggestions for *Deadmistress*: Alice DeLana and Karen Riem, the original readers; Margaret Carroll. Marcia Hall, Nancy Hoffman, Sara Lapuk, Tom Ratliff and Steve Thomson, all readers of version two. Thanks also to Billie Bernstein who wrote me my first fan letter, to Baird Jarman whose comments helped me move from the first version to the second, and to Jill Susannah Shmurak who was instrumental in giving this book a name And finally, my eternal gratitude to my husband, Steve Shmurak, for his unswerving support.

CAST OF CHARACTERS

AT WINTONBURY ACADEMY:

Sabena Lazlo: *head of Wintonbury Academy for Girls (WAG)*

Jane Ackerman: *Sabena's loyal and efficient secretary*

Elaine Dodgson: *teacher of drama at WAG for over 20 years*

John deHavilland: *teacher of history*

Margaret "Granny" Smith: *assistant academic dean*

Harry Trout: *teacher of mathematics at WAG for over 20 years*

Louise Trout: *Harry's long-suffering wife*

Alan Lyons: *assistant head of WAG and dean of students*

Beth Lyons: *Alan's wife and director of dormitory*

Rob Fleming: *poet and chair of the English department*

Barbara Gordon: *teacher of chemistry*

Melinda Collingswood: *chairperson of the Board of Trustees*

Mandy Lewis, Nini Westmore, Tiffany Wood, Shauna Thompson, Punkin Brady, Liza Ledyard: *students at WAG*

Phil Harbison, Laraine Marshall, Chuck Harris: *other staff at WAG*

AT METROPOLITAN UNIVERSITY:

Susan Lombardi: *professor of education, former teacher at WAG*

Mark Goldin: *student and former private investigator*

Nanette Lehman: *chair of the department of education*

Rick Benedetto, Laurie Nash: *professors of education*

Scott Jeffries: *chair of the department of art*

Harold Simonds: *dean of the school of education*

ELSEWHERE:

Michael Buckler: *Susan's husband*

Caz Czaikowski: *officer in Wintonbury Police department*

Harvey Konigsberg, Richard Westcott: *figures from Sabena's past*

CHAPTER ONE

"I met Murder on the way —"
Percy Bysshe Shelley, *The Mask of Anarchy*

I was trapped in morning traffic when I first heard the news about Sabena. Driving to the university that January morning, I found myself — for the first time — regretting my decision not to own a cell phone. Her death hadn't made it into the morning newspaper, which lay on the seat beside me, and here I was, stuck in my car with no way to get more information than the eight A.M. news report had to give:

"Sabena Lazlo, headmistress of the exclusive Wintonbury Academy for Girls, was found dead in her office early this morning, apparently from a gunshot wound to the head. The Wintonbury Police are investigating and have not said whether the death is a suicide or a homicide. More later. Now back to you, Bruce."

I pounded the steering wheel in frustration. Not only was I going to be late for my meeting, but then I would have to sit through an hour of pompous blather before I could call anyone to learn more about Sabena. Suicide? Not Sabena. Surely her egotism and posturing had finally driven someone over the edge. A student? A teacher? Perhaps a parent?

Yesterday — I had just been to Wintonbury yesterday, doing my research. Everything had seemed normal: students running about, late to class, teachers griping as they stood in line for the copy machine. Could that all have changed overnight?

What would Wintonbury be like today? I wanted to turn my car around and head to the campus, but I had duties at the university that I couldn't shirk. I thought about how an important part of my life was still at Wintonbury; not just friends on the faculty, but my research as well.

A newcomer to the university in my mid-forties, I had been anxious to carve out a niche for myself that would serve as a "research agenda." Building on my experience as a former teacher at Wintonbury, I soon found that niche by doing research on girls' behavior in the classroom. Last week, I had spent my afternoons visiting classrooms at the coed Eastford Prep; this week and next, I was scheduled for visits to Wintonbury.

It had been strange being back there as a visitor. Everything was so familiar, yet I was not a part of it. I had taken in the beauty of the campus with renewed delight, but I'd avoided going into the administration building. I hadn't wanted to talk to Sabena, although she had been atypically gracious about giving her official permission for me to be there.

Finally, the traffic thinned out, and I drove as fast as possible down the backroads to Metropolitan University. I found an empty space in the parking lot and rushed to my meeting in the ugly, cinder block building that housed the School of Education.

As a rule, I find it difficult to sit through meetings. That morning it was intolerable. I was aching to go to my office and call someone for details, but whom? Surely, the Wintonbury switchboard would be buzzing all morning. My friends on the faculty would be busy with hysterical students, who never needed an excuse for melodrama. It could hardly be business as usual at Wintonbury Academy today.

A professor from another department, whom I'd only met once before, was droning on and on about vision statements and long-term objectives. I looked at my watch for the third time.

"And so I think we need an ad hoc committee to examine these issues," he finally concluded.

"Good idea," agreed the dean. "Volunteers?"

Hands were going up all around me. I looked down at my non-existent notes and tried to be inconspicuous. My schedule — and my sanity — couldn't handle another committee.

The meeting finally ended.

"Susan," asked Dean Simonds, calling me back as I headed for the door. "Didn't you know that woman who was killed last night?"

"Yes," I said. "I used to work at Wintonbury Academy. She was my boss for three years. I, uh, didn't know her all that well though."

I didn't say that I had left Wintonbury because of Sabena. I really didn't want to have to explain my relationship with her. And besides, I was chagrined at not having any more information.

"Whew," he replied, a smile playing on his lips. "I hope all your ex-bosses don't meet with a similar fate."

"I don't think you have to worry about that," I said, smiling in return and backing through his office door. As I walked down the hallway, I decided to call my husband to see if he had heard anything about Sabena.

At my office, students were waiting three-deep to see me.

"Where is everybody, Marie?" I grumbled.

She just shrugged. "Classes don't start till tomorrow. No one comes in this early but us secretaries." It was nine-thirty.

From the smoke seeping out from under the door of Rick Benedetto's office, I knew she was lying. Poor Marie. He had probably told her to lie for him. Rick hated students.

"Okay," I said in my most professional manner, "I'll take you one at a time."

"Doctor Lombardi," sighed the first student, who came in flinging herself into a chair opposite mine. "I have been to three offices so far, and no one can tell me which courses I need. The dean's secretary sent me to the history department and the history department sent me to the grad school and ...."

She wasn't a young woman; in her late thirties or early forties, I thought. She had probably raised a family and was now returning to college, like so many students at Metropolitan University.

"All right," I said. "I know this place can be hard to deal with sometimes. Let's see what we can do."

And so the morning passed. If I had intended to do any work it would have been impossible. At noon, I declared myself on lunch break, closed the door to my office, and dialed my home phone number. It was great having a husband who worked at home, I often told my colleagues. Worked at home! What a euphemism, I thought. He plays with his computer all day, while I deal with committees and anxious students and agonize over dead headmistresses.

"Swash, what have you heard about Sabena?"

His real name is Michael Buckler, but I haven't called him Michael in the twenty-five years that I've known him. I'd met and married Swash soon after college graduation, when we were both penniless graduate students. Then his maiden aunt, Rachel, had died, leaving her nephew a surprisingly large inheritance. Through savvy investment, Swash turned Aunt Rachel's money into a larger fortune and hasn't had a regular job since.

"Ah, so you've heard! I wondered when the news would penetrate your halls of ivy."

"Ivy, indeed." He knew what Metropolitan's campus looked like — there wasn't a sprig of ivy anywhere, just cinder block and concrete. "Come on, Swash, what are they saying?"

"The last report on the radio said that the gun hasn't been found. They're calling it a homicide."

"Homicide! Oh, my God. Anything else?"

"That's it. I'm not really listening to every word. Besides, what do you care? You don't work for her anymore."

"But a lot of my friends still do! And I knew her. I never knew anyone who was murdered before!"

"Too bad she wasn't murdered years ago. Before she came to Wintonbury."

"Oh God, you're so heartless. And you're no help at all. Should I call someone?"

"Susan, why not leave your friends at Wintonbury alone for a while? They have their hands full. Besides, aren't you seeing Elaine for dinner tonight?"

"Geez, I'd almost forgotten that. I hope she doesn't cancel our date."

"Yeah, you might die of curiosity. Seriously, Susan, stay out of it. You're not a part of the school anymore."

"Guess I better go now. Students are pounding at my door."

I hate it when he's being sensible.

CHAPTER TWO

"The endearing elegance of female friendship."
Samuel Johnson, *Rasselas*

Elaine and I had been good friends from my first days at Wintonbury, and we had kept up our friendship through the years by meeting a few times a month for dinner. For the last few years, our meeting place had been an elegant Italian restaurant called Buonarotti's.

Elaine teaches drama at Wintonbury Academy. For a brief time in her youth, she had appeared off-Broadway, but her New York career was cut short when she married a handsome attorney who brought her back to New England. Finding herself a bit further off-Broadway than she had planned, she made the best of it by creating an outstanding drama program at Wintonbury.

That was over twenty years ago. Her children had grown up, her husband had left her to marry a young lawyer from his office, and Elaine was still teaching adolescent thespians at Wintonbury. But her sense of drama and her youthful energy were intact, and she still turned heads as she swept into the restaurant.

Elaine was willowy and tall, and emphasized the fact by wearing her pre-Raphaelite red hair piled high upon her head. An enormous amber necklace and high-necked black dress completed the look.

"Dear, dear Susan! I'm so glad to see you! We've been having the most ghastly time of it! As I'm sure you can imagine." She sighed as she slipped gracefully into her chair.

"Yes," I said, "I've been imagining all sorts of things. Tell me what you know."

"I know nothing, I'm afraid. As far as the police are concerned, Wintonbury faculty are all suspects, I think."

"You must know something — more than those of us outside the school, at least," I insisted.

"We're being kept totally in the dark by the police, I assure you," she replied. "But most of us have been busy making up theories by the carload. Have you spoken to John?"

"No, I was afraid to call anyone this afternoon."

John deHavilland was a history teacher at Wintonbury and a dear friend.

"Well, he seems to be everyone's favorite candidate for prime suspect because of some silly speech he made at faculty meeting. People say he threatened Sabena."

"My God. What could have provoked that?"

"Something about faculty housing." Elaine opened her menu and looked down at it for a moment, then she smiled up at me. "Actually, I skipped that faculty meeting so my information is very secondhand. You should get the real story from John himself."

"I will. But John threatening someone, even Sabena — I can't imagine that."

"Of course. You and I know that he's just an old windbag! He might bluster a bit, but he'd never actually do anything like murder."

"If I know that and so do you, why don't the others?"

"Frankly, I think some people would like it to be John. He does come on a bit strong, you must admit. It turns a lot of people, less hardy than we are, against him."

"So who's your candidate, Elaine?"

"I've been asking myself that. I know who I'd like it to be: Harry Trout. If the police would just arrest him, the whole school would be better off."

"Do you seriously suspect old Harry?"

"No, of course not." She waved her hand dismissively. "He's probably as ineffectual as a murderer as he is as a teacher. I'd just like to see him behind bars because of what he does to the girls."

Harry Trout was well known as the most boring teacher at Wintonbury. He taught mathematics, and although Wintonbury boasted some very gifted math teachers, Harry was not one of them. Not content to just bore the students to tears, he was also reputed to humiliate the weaker students in his class in a very public manner. He'd been at the school even longer than Elaine had, and had intimidated two former headmistresses sufficiently to keep his job despite repeated parental complaints.

"I think Sabena was working up her courage to fire him at last," continued Elaine. "Too bad she didn't get around to it sooner."

The waiter came to take our orders. He was new at Buonarotti's and seemed as captivated by Elaine as all men were. Expressing heartfelt approval of her menu choices, he also insisted on bringing us extra garlic bread. When he finally left our table, I brought the conversation back to Sabena.

"Really, Elaine, can you think of anyone who might have a reason to kill her?"

"Let's see. What about that little sleaze Rob Fleming? I think he's having an affair with a student again. You remember the last one?"

Unfortunately, I did. "Could Sabena have found out?"

Elaine raised one perfectly penciled eyebrow. "If she didn't know, she was the only one on campus who didn't."

"Would she have fired him for that? He certainly deserves it."

"No, he's the star of the English department, with all that poetry he's published. And he is an excellent teacher, I hear. She'd never get rid of him."

She broke off a piece of bread and nibbled it thoughtfully. "Not to mention that firing him for having an affair would be an interesting moral position for Sabena to take, given her little romance with Alan." Alan Lyons was the Dean of Students and Sabena's second-in-command. He was also married with two young children and an apartment on campus.

"I suppose so, but Alan is at least a consenting adult. Those poor smitten seniors that Rob takes advantage of ...."

"It's funny they never complain though," mused Elaine. "I guess he's pretty good. Maybe I should give him a whirl!"

I choked on my garlic bread. The thought of tall, elegant Elaine with that pretentious little worm was more than I could bear.

"One of these days there will be a complaint against Rob," I said. "And the school will be in a sorry mess, with everyone claiming they didn't know about his sordid affairs."

"Perhaps you're right," she sighed. "But that doesn't give him a motive for murder now, does it?" She paused. "Susan, I argued with Sabena the day before she was murdered. Do you think that will make me a suspect?"

"No, of course not. What were you arguing with her about?"

"She was planning to cancel the Shakespeare festival in the spring! She said we didn't have the money anymore to be so extravagant, and besides she thought it was old-hat! Can you believe that?"

Her eyes filled with tears of indignation. The spring Shakespeare festival was Elaine's creation and her *raison d'etre*. She spent untold hours each April coaching the girls on their diction, designing Elizabethan costumes, planning publicity. It was one of the things that made Wintonbury Academy famous, and Elaine along with it.

I made sympathetic noises and wondered just what Elaine would do if she felt her festival threatened. "So what did you tell her?"

"Well, of course, I said I would resign. What else could I do? Wintonbury Academy without Shakespeare on the lawn? I simply couldn't stay under those circumstances!"

The main course came, and we interrupted our conversation until the hovering waiter was satisfied that Elaine was happy with her meal.

"Did you mean it? Would you resign?"

"I certainly meant it at the time, but now I don't know. At my age, who would hire me?"

"Any of the local schools would be overjoyed to get you, Elaine!"

"Yes, but they already have drama teachers. They don't need me, do they?" She paused, her eyes focused somewhere beyond our table. "Well, Sabena's gone, and the festival is safe, at least for now." With a little satisfied smile, she sipped her wine.

"How about a student?" I asked.

"Well, I admit our students do have some strange, and sometimes scary, traditions, but murdering the headmistress has never been one of them," she replied. "Besides, I think most of them had a sort of grudging respect for her."

"Or a parent? Could she have angered one of them?" I persisted.

"Well, that old biddy, Mrs. Archer, was on campus yesterday. Remember her?"

I nodded. I had recognized Mrs. Archer's silver Mercedes in the parking lot the day before. It was hard to miss, with its vanity plate proclaiming MOMARCH.

"She's sent three daughters to Wintonbury, and each one has been more stupid than the last! The latest one was Marcy. She couldn't even cheat intelligently. She was caught last week for handing in a paper that her sister Missy had written three years ago!"

I groaned. I had taught Missy. "My goodness, Missy was certainly no literary light either, was she?"

"See what I mean? Each one more stupid than the last! Missy at least did her own wretched work. We're well rid of Marcy. I only hope they send the fourth one someplace else."

"Who was the one before Missy? I don't remember her."

"Let's see. Was it Margie? Yes, I think that's right: Margie, Missy, Marcy and...."

"Oh God, don't tell me! Muffy?"

"I'm afraid so." We dissolved into shrieks of laughter, causing the other patrons to give us curious stares. The infatuated waiter came over and inquired if we needed some dessert. It was clear, even to him, that we had had enough wine.

CHAPTER THREE

"Let schoolmasters puzzle their brains
With grammar, and nonsense and learning;
Good liquor, I stoutly maintain,
Gives genius a better discerning."
Oliver Goldsmith, *She Stoops to Conquer*

Elaine and I lingered over the chocolate decadence and the remaining wine, laughing and reminiscing about our days at Wintonbury together.

"Remember when the whole faculty taught in bizarre costumes for a whole day?" I said. "I was a floozie. I remember teaching all my classes in Brooklynese and watching the girls' eyes pop out as they realized they had to take notes while I said things like 'Krebs soycle' for 'Krebs cycle.' You were a beatnik that day, I think."

"Ah, yes, I remember that," she said, tilting her wine glass to get at the last few drops. "I loved your costume and the way you teased your hair out to unheard of heights. And the perfume! Didn't you douse yourself with it?"

I nodded. "Yes, I used up a whole sample of Shalimar I found in the back of a dresser drawer. Certainly gave the chem lab a whole new smell."

"But none of us would come near you that day." Elaine chuckled softly. "And remember when we filled dear old Mrs. Worthington's office, floor to ceiling, with the girls' stuffed animals? Wasn't that a wonderful prank?" Marian Worthington had been the head of Wintonbury Academy when I first arrived.

"Can you imagine doing that to Sabena?" I asked. "No one would ever have dared to play a prank like that on her."

Elaine smiled mischievously. "Some of us *have* played pranks on Sabena, now and then."

"Yes, but she had no sense of humor!"

"You're right about that, of course. She was much too self-absorbed to see anything funny in life. Wintonbury certainly was more fun in the P.S. days."

"P.S? Oh, pre-Sabena? Or should it be B.S. for Before Sabena? After all, P.S. could also be post-Sabena."

"Which, thankfully, it is now. Oh, that's really a horrible thing to say. I should be ashamed!"

"Elaine, I just thought of something. If Wintonbury could have a time pre-Sabena, then Sabena had a time pre-Wintonbury."

"And so?" She looked at me quizzically.

"What I mean," I continued, "is that Sabena had a life before she came to Wintonbury. What if someone from her pre-Wintonbury days murdered her? What do you know about Sabena before she came here?"

"Hmm, not a lot. She never revealed much. Except of course to tell you how she had single-handledly saved Tamarac Academy from bankruptcy. Or to remind you what a brilliant student she had been at Columbia and Penn."

"Wasn't there some gossip about an ex-husband?"

"Actually, there was gossip about *two* ex-husbands, but I don't know where that rumor started."

"Two ex-husbands. What a life the woman led." I sipped my wine and mused about Sabena and her relationships with men.

As if reading my thoughts, Elaine said, "She probably had quite a few men in her past, I think."

"But Elaine, don't you think her past might be the key? Couldn't this open a whole new side to the police investigation?"

"Susan, I'm not sure that any of those rumors was true. And besides, shouldn't we leave all of this to the professionals?" She slurred the *s*'s in the last word just a bit. Then she yawned. "Oh dear, I can't believe we've occupied this table for three and a half hours! We'd better pay our check."

On the — thankfully short — drive home, I congratulated myself on how clever I'd been to realize that the pool of suspects could be extended beyond Wintonbury Academy. I hoped someone on the Wintonbury police force was thinking the same way.

Swash was in bed reading when I came in. I gave him a quick kiss and summarized the conversation with Elaine.

"Poor John," he said. "It's hard to believe the police could actually suspect him."

"Yes," I agreed. "But Elaine isn't taking John's plight too seriously. Actually, she isn't taking Sabena's death all that hard either."

"Well, people have peculiar ways of reacting to death, especially sudden death. Perhaps it will hit her later — after the wine has worn off."

"She did have a lot to drink tonight," I admitted.

"Well, that's what I've come to expect when you and Elaine get together. So what will you do about your research this week?" he asked. "Surely you can't go to Wintonbury tomorrow?"

"Elaine says that the Board of Trustees is determined to keep the school up and running. There will be a special assembly tomorrow morning. Counselors will be available for the girls and faculty, and then classes will go on in the afternoon."

"But those classes won't be valid ones to study as part of your research...."

"Depends on what you mean by research."

He gave me a worried look. "Susan, you know you should stay out of this. You're going up for tenure at Metropolitan next year. You should be doing your research and publishing articles, shouldn't you?"

"Yes, I should."

"And you don't know the first thing about criminal investigation, do you?"

"No, I don't."

"And you're going to get involved anyway, aren't you?"

"Yes, I am."

He sighed.

"Swash, don't be angry with me! Help me. I'm still a part of Wintonbury, even if I don't actually work there. So many of my friends still do, and I have such happy memories of the place. We were like one big family...."

"Until Sabena came," he reminded me.

"I know, I know. But...."

"I think I'll attend the special assembly with you tomorrow."

I eyed him suspiciously. "Because you don't want me to get involved?"

"No, because, like you, I never knew anyone who was murdered before."

"Aha! You're as curious as I am!"

"Susan, no one is as curious as you are. But, yes, I am sort of interested in how people are reacting to this."

Sort of interested was an understatement, I decided. It took a lot to get Swash out of the house. Since his Aunt Rachel had died, leaving him that not-so-modest fortune, Swash had stayed at home, performing acts of arcane financial wizardry on his computer, and seldom leaving to go anywhere.

"This assembly isn't really for outsiders, you know," I said.

"And you and I aren't outsiders, are we? We were both involved members of the school community for years." Swash had attended the yearly faculty Christmas party and a few of Elaine's plays, but for him, that was major involvement.

"I guess you're right. We can at least try to get you in. So you can come with me to Wintonbury in the morning, and I'll stay for the classes in the afternoon."

"Sure, we'll take two cars. Oh, speaking of cars, your daughter is making a case again for bringing a car to campus next year. There's a long e-mail waiting for you downstairs."

"*My* daughter? I think you had something to do with her existence. Approximately eighteen years ago, if memory serves."

Our daughter Joanne, happily settled into college life in western Massachusetts, is one of Swash's greatest sources of pride. She only becomes my daughter when she is whiny or demanding.

"Well, that e-mail can wait till tomorrow," I said. "I've pretty much had it for tonight."

Swash sighed, then smiled that delicious smile of his, his hazel eyes dancing. "Well, as a matter of fact, there may be some other e-mails of interest downstairs. Of interest especially to those with insatiable curiosities about matters that don't concern them."

"Swash! What do you mean?"

"Ahem. I was surfing the Net tonight and ...."

"No! Sabena's got a homepage on the Web?"

"Will you be quiet, woman! No, there's no Sabena homepage, but I did find...." He paused for effect. I didn't interrupt this time. "An independent school discussion list and...."

"Yes?"

"I sent a message into cyberspace asking for anyone who knew Sabena to e-mail you."

"And?"

"Well, that's it. I just sent the message a few hours ago."

"Swash, this is the information age! We might have ten answers by now!" And I ran down the stairs to the spacious study that we share. The e-mail directory on my computer indicated more than a dozen replies to Swash's message. It was going to be a late night. I hoped my students wouldn't notice the dark circles under my eyes the next day.

CHAPTER FOUR

"Gossip is mischievous, light and easy to raise,
but grievous to bear and hard to get rid of.
No gossip ever dies away entirely, if many people
voice it: it too is a kind of divinity."
Hesiod, *Works and Days*

The first few replies were useless, a mixture of condolences to her friends and indignation that such a thing as murder could happen to anyone in the cloistered world of independent schools. None of the writers seemed to have actually known Sabena. But message number six read:

> Dear Susan,
>   I heard with sadness and dismay about the death of Dr. Lazlo. Sabena and I were in the same workshop for new heads of independent schools at Columbia University several years ago. She was a strong and vital presence in the workshop. If there is anything I can do to help her friends or her school, please do not hesitate to contact me.
> Mary Littleton Farmer
> Head, Capital Oaks School

Hmm, I thought, the first really positive thing I've heard about Sabena in a long time. But not much help. I skimmed two more generic condolence messages, and then:

Dear Susan,

    I taught with Sabena many years ago at a school in New York. Not to speak ill of the dead, but she was only a so-so teacher and a terrible, back-stabbing colleague. Of course, she was going through a divorce at the time, but that only made me feel sorry for her husband. Sorry, can't remember his name, but I do know it wasn't Lazlo.

Jack Lonnigan

Social Studies Dept, Grant-Burke School

So she did have at least one husband! I quickly typed a reply:

Dear Jack,

    How long ago and at what school in New York did you know Sabena? Thanks for any further info you can provide.

Susan Lombardi

I read on, hoping for some news about husband number two. Instead, I found this:

Dear Susan,

    I am currently Dean of Students at Tamarac Academy, which is, I'm sure you know, the school where Sabena served as Academic Dean prior to becoming Head of Wintonbury Academy. I'm afraid I did not find Sabena to be a very gracious colleague, nor a very honest one. I think it is terrible that she was murdered, but I cannot say that we at Tamarac have missed her very much.

Jeannette Richardson

Tamarac Academy

I clicked Reply and wrote :

Dear Jeannette,
    I know what you mean by the 'not very gracious' part, but can you be more specific about what you mean by 'nor a very honest one'?
Susan Lombardi

There were three more useless messages and then:

Susan,
    That woman was a harpy from hell. I should know—she stole my husband. Of course, she couldn't keep him long either. I would have liked to pull the trigger myself, but I never had the nerve.
Kathy Marchand
Briar Hills Day School

Was this woman talking about husband number one or number two? How frustrating that people couldn't be more explicit in their messages! I zapped back a reply:

Kathy,
    What school was she at when you knew her? What was her (your) husband's name? Do you know where he is now?
Susan Lombardi

It was late, and I still hadn't read my daughter's e-mail. I never imagined that I would get any more answers before I went to bed, but then there was a happy little beep on my machine. Jack Lonnigan, bless him, was still on-line.

Susan,

It was in the 1970s at the Marston School in Manhattan. Sabena was just out of UPenn with her master's degree, and getting rid of her husband, whom she felt she had outgrown. I think he was an accountant. Still can't recall his name. Will let you know if I remember. I'll also check with my wife tomorrow—she's got a better memory for names than I do.

Jack

Thank you, I typed, along with encouragement to keep thinking, then I waited for more beeps. None came. Cyberspace — or at least that small fraction of it who belonged to the Indep-L discussion group — had closed up shop for the night. After all, school folk had to be in their classrooms and offices early the next morning.

Swash was already asleep when I came back upstairs, full of news. I was tempted to wake him but thought better of it. Instead, I stared at the ceiling for most of the night, listening to Swash's breathing. My mind was racing with possibilities. I had definitely confirmed the existence of one ex-husband. Whether Kathy Marchand's ex-husband was the same one Jack Lonnigan had mentioned or the second one, I still didn't know. But I would know that soon, as well as his name.

CHAPTER FIVE

"Every murderer is probably somebody's old friend."
Agatha Christie, *The Mysterious Affair at Styles*

It was eight the next morning when Swash and I drove to the Wintonbury campus. I was sure that we would be stopped by police as we entered, but the only one on duty at the gate was Chuck Harris, the old security guard, who recognized both of us and waved our cars into the visitors' parking lot.

Wintonbury Academy's campus is idyllic. Located just across the street from the village green in the picture-postcard New England town of Wintonbury, Connecticut, it extends back from the street for acre after rolling acre. Wintonbury Brook, glazed with ice in the winter, bisects the campus. Buildings from the many architectural periods since the school's founding in the mid-nineteenth century are set like jewels against the hills. Georgian brick dormitories and Victorian art studios face ultra-modern laboratories. The new gymnasium, glistening with steel and glass, proclaims itself the best that alumnae money can buy. And, somehow, it all combines harmoniously into a cozy, welcoming milieu.

Swash and I hurried across the campus, past the Head's House, over the well-sanded footbridge to the building that housed the theatre. "Elaine's Theatre" was how I thought of it. We craned our necks to find seats in the packed auditorium.

"Look," I said. "There's John sitting all alone. Let's go join him."

Indeed, John deHavilland seemed to be sitting in his own world, several empty seats on either side of him. Could the entire Wintonbury Academy community be treating him as a pariah? He sat staring straight ahead, his big bearlike body erect, his usually mobile face frozen into a mask. I gave his arm a pat as I took the seat next to him. And I thought I saw one of his eyes wink at me in reply.

Melinda Collingswood, chairperson of the Board of Trustees, was up front at the podium. Tall and broad-shouldered, she looked sadly out at the sea of faces before her. Years of playing field hockey and tennis, followed by running a small but prosperous public relations firm, had not prepared her for this. She shook her graying pageboy a few times, took a deep breath, and then began the ceremony.

"Thank you all for coming. We are here this morning to pay tribute to our beloved headmistress, Sabena Laszlo. Let me first ask Phil Harbison, the school chaplain, to come up."

Phil, bushy-haired and bespectacled, rose from his seat in the front row and walked determinedly to the podium.

"We come together today to remember Sabena Lazlo," he said. "Let us begin with a minute of silent reflection or prayer, as our individual consciences dictate."

All heads obediently bowed. I raised my eyes, however, to look around at the audience. Some of the students were crying quietly into wads of tissue. Jane Ackerman, Sabena's secretary, sat in the front row, sobbing into her lace-trimmed handkerchief. Next to her was the assistant academic dean, Margaret Smith, fondly known as "Granny." Granny was patting Jane's shoulder with her plump, little hand. The rest of the faculty occupied the back rows and seemed somber but relatively unmoved.

The minute was up. Phil sat down and was immediately replaced at the podium by Granny Smith. She was dressed, as she usually was, in a plain, dark-colored dress, but her customary warm smile was missing.

"Good morning everyone," she began, speaking quietly. "The trustees and I thought it best to run this like a Quaker meeting. As any of you thinks of something you want to say, or any moment in your life with Sabena Lazlo that you want to remember, please rise to your feet and share it with us."

There was a long silence as everyone looked around, each hoping someone else would go first. When it was clear that no one was willing to begin, Granny stepped into the breach.

"I remember Dr. Lazlo's first day at Wintonbury," she said. "She was moving into her office, and I came down the hall to help her. It was a hot July day, and we ended up sitting under that poor excuse of an air conditioner, unpacking books all afternoon. And we spoke about all her ideas for changing how things were done here. I didn't always agree with her, but I respected her."

"And I remember her cheering for the team at our field hockey games," put in one of the girls, rising to her feet. "She, you know, was one of the loudest cheerers. The field hockey team is going to miss her a lot."

"Yes," said another. "And she always supported the dance group too. She sat in the front row at every performance. And she always gave us a standing ovation."

Several other girls, probably seniors, rose to speak about Sabena. They each contributed an anecdote, but I noticed that none of them said that they liked her. A few faculty members gave carefully worded reminiscences, also avoiding any mention of their feelings.

"This was not a beloved leader," Swash whispered to me at one point.

"Shh," I said. "I don't want to miss any of this."

Finally, it was over, and Melinda Collingswood strode back to the podium.

"Thank you, everyone, for that moving celebration of the life of Sabena Lazlo," she said. "Now I just want to reassure everyone. The Board of Trustees has voted to keep the school open. Classes will resume B Period this morning, and you will follow your regular Wednesday schedule. We have increased security at the school with the help of the Wintonbury town police, and no one is in any danger. If you are sincerely too upset to go to class, please see one of the school's counselors for help. Otherwise, we will expect you to be in class. Wintonbury girls — and faculty — you all know that we must carry on with our lives. Dr. Lazlo would have wanted it that way."

As people started to file out of the auditorium, I grabbed John's arm.

"What did you think of that?" I asked.

"Bunch of hypocrites," he replied. "Not one of them liked her."

"Whew, that was pretty evident," said Swash.

"And see how everyone is avoiding me? It's like they don't want to be tainted with knowing me."

"Oh, John," I said. "It can't be that bad."

"Believe me, it is. Don't you know you may be speaking to the 'Prime Suspect' this very minute?" I could hear the capital letters in his voice. John knew how to use that voice of his. It made him a captivating story-teller and a brilliant history teacher. I could feel a dramatic monolog coming on.

"What does that mean?"

"Well, my dear, it seems I made an impassioned speech at the faculty meeting last week, and accused Sabena of destroying faculty morale and dragging the school down with it. I'm afraid I got a bit vehement."

"And so? Surely, other people were upset with her too. What crime against humanity had the Empress committed this time?"

"She was about to recommend to the trustees that the school sell off all the faculty houses at the end of the year. That would force all of us who live on campus to move over the summer. You know I can't afford to buy a house as nice as the one I live in now."

"Well, of course. But that goes for a lot of people. Why should that make you the number one suspect?"

"Yes, well, it also seems that I threatened her."

"You what?" asked Swash. John is one of the most nonviolent people we know — a caring teacher and a nurturing, single father.

"I honestly don't remember what I said. I was so furious. I think I said something about stopping her. Of course, I meant I would talk to the Board of Trustees myself and try to dissuade them from selling the houses, but some of the civic-minded faculty of Wintonbury heard a threat to Sabena in there, and have informed the police of it."

"No one in their right mind could possibly suspect you, John." I reached up to pat his tweed-covered shoulder. He and Swash each towered a foot above my five foot two.

"I don't know. The police were certainly asking me a lot of questions. And of course, I have no alibi. I was home in bed and Jason was fast asleep at the supposed time of the murder. Besides, no one at Wintonbury Academy is in their right minds at this moment. We're all in shock. And, of course, at the best of times, some of us are barely sane. You remember what it's like."

We looked around to find that we three were the only people left in the theatre. All the others had left to seek shelter in their classrooms or dormitories.

John looked nervously at his watch. "Swash, good to see you, but I've got to get to class. Susan, you'll be coming to American History later?"

Swash and John exchanged good-byes, and John hurried away. I gave Swash a peck on the cheek as he left and went off to visit Jane Ackerman.

The January sun shone wanly on the snow-topped buildings and ice-trimmed trees as I trudged up the hill to the administration building. Girls in their uniforms of down-filled vests, Ivy League college sweatshirts, and jeans, scurried by on their way to appointments with teachers or counselors. Things appeared as they'd always been.

CHAPTER SIX

"High school is closer to the core of the American
experience than anything else I can think of."
Kurt Vonnegut, Jr.
Introduction to *Our Time is Now: Notes from the
High School Underground*

But then I entered the administration building. There at
the front was Sabena's office, marked off with yellow scene-of-
the-crime tape. A Wintonbury police officer was stationed at the
door. I shuddered and went across the hall to Jane Ackerman's
office. It was empty.

The lights were on, so I assumed that Jane would be back
soon. I waited in the hallway looking at bulletin boards covered
with news clippings about the accomplishments of Wintonbury
girls and Wintonbury faculty. Nothing about the murder, of
course.

I was in the middle of reading a *New York Times* article about
the first female CEO of a large media conglomerate when two
long-haired girls walked by, absorbed in conversation.

"So I'm like, what do you want from me? And he's like, well,
I don't know, what do *you* want from me?"

"You need to break up with that slime, Mandy. You can do
so much better than him."

One of the girls noticed me standing in the hall. "Hi, can
we help you?" she asked sweetly, her whole manner changing.
Wintonbury girls are always polite to strangers, if not always to
each other.

"No, that's okay. I'm waiting for Mrs. Ackerman."

"Well, you won't have to wait long — she's always here. Especially now with the Emp—with Dr. Lazlo gone, she's kind of running the school." The two girls exchanged looks, and one suppressed a giggle. "Are you here about the murder? We're not supposed to talk about it...."

"No, I'm not here about that," I replied, glancing across the hall at the police officer, who didn't appear to be listening. "I'm doing some educational research here at Wintonbury. I'll just wait here for Mrs. Ackerman to get back. Don't worry about me. I'm fine just waiting by myself. I used to work here."

"Really? What's your name? When were you here?" She brushed her pale hair out of her face, revealing large blue eyes.

"I'm Susan Lombardi. I was here for ten years. I left five years ago."

"Um, I think maybe I've heard of you," mused the one named Mandy.

"Wait, I think you taught my sister math," said the blonde.

"It was biology or chemistry," I corrected, "But what was her name?"

"My sister? Lauren Westmore. I'm Nini Westmore."

"Sure, I remember Lauren. What's she doing?"

"Oh, she's at Vassar. Majoring in drama."

"That's great. Give her my regards."

I had no trouble conjuring up an image of Lauren Westmore. Lauren had been one of my favorite students: not a quick learner, but a hard worker, determined to understand for herself and not just for the grade. I remembered, too, that Lauren had gotten into trouble with her dorm directors over a nude male poster she'd hung in her room. I had tried to champion her rights — one more thing I'd done to antagonize Sabena. Eventually, we'd worked out a face-saving compromise; the poster came down, but Michelangelo's David went up in its place.

Nini, with her flaxen hair and azure eyes, could have been Lauren's twin. If I hadn't been so distracted by Sabena's death, I would have guessed the relationship.

They wandered off, leaving me thinking about how short the collective memory of a high school is. I'd been gone only five years, but none of the students had any idea who I was. I was ancient history.

As I stood there feeling superfluous, Jane Ackerman returned. She looked haggard, and her eyes were red from crying at the assembly. But she was still the efficient secretary and bustled into her office, peering down at some papers and not noticing me standing outside. A second later, she poked her head out.

"Susan! What are you doing here?"

"Well, actually, I'm still doing my research on girls' behavior in the classroom, and I thought...."

"Yes, I guess the rest of the world must still be going on about its business. Come in, Susan, and talk to me."

With a baleful look at the Wintonbury policeman, Jane closed the door to her office. I sat down in a chair near her desk.

Jane looked at me and groaned. "This place is crazy. We're trying to continue as if nothing's happened. But there's Sabena's office all closed off with yellow tape, and she's...." Tears started to roll down her withered cheeks. Someone, at least, regretted Sabena's passing.

"How's the school holding up?"

"Well, nineteen families have taken their girls out of the school. They're worried about a killer running loose on the campus. I guess I can't blame them, but...."

"You don't think this was a random killing, do you, Jane?"

"I almost wish it were. But no, I think someone hated Sabena enough to kill her. That's it, plain and simple."

"What do the police think?"

She sniffed, drawing her slight body rigidly straight in her desk chair. "They aren't telling us anything, of course. That policeman across the hall won't even let me go into Sabena's office to get what I need to keep this school running."

"From what I hear, you're doing an amazing job of keeping things going."

"Oh, thank you, Susan. We are trying valiantly — Granny and Alan and myself. I just wish we knew who did this terrible, terrible thing. And why."

"What do you think happened, Jane?"

"I keep asking myself, did Sabena do something different on Monday — something that provoked this? I just don't know."

"Was anything special about that day?"

"No, just the usual round of meetings and appointments."

"Jane, do you remember who Sabena had appointments with on Monday?" I hoped her low regard for the police would keep her talking to me.

"Well, no, I don't really remember, and the police have taken away her appointment calendar."

I tried to hide my disappointment. "Can you remember any of them?"

Jane looked at me somewhat dubiously. Then a conspiratorial smile spread across her face.

"Susan, I shouldn't really tell you this, but...."

"Yes?"

"I keep a duplicate calendar in my desk drawer. I use it to schedule appointments for Sabena — used to use it, I mean — and then I would put them in the calendar on her desk."

"Sounds like a very efficient way to do things," I said.

"I tried," sighed Jane.

"Do you think I could take a look at the calendar?" I asked, trying not to appear too eager.

"Well now, I'm not sure — is it considered evidence? Even if it's just a copy of what the police already have?"

"No, I don't think so. As long as they have the original, what difference could it make?"

Jane shrugged. "You're probably right. What difference could it make if you and I just have a peek?"

I think I held my breath the entire time it took Jane to retrieve the calendar from the top drawer.

"Well, here it is. Do you really think it's one of these people, Susan?"

"Jane, I don't know. But it's a place to start, don't you think?"

We huddled together as I read her perfect penmanship:

9 A.M.	Staff meeting
10 A.M.	Harry Trout
10:15 A.M.	Elaine Dodgson
11 A.M.	Rob Fleming
12 noon	Lunch with Mrs. Archer
1 P.M.	Tiffany Wood
1:30 P.M.	Punkin Brady
2 P.M.	Liza Ledyard
2:30 P M.	Shauna Thompson
3 PM	Faculty meeting

"And did all these people keep their appointments that day?" I asked.

She thought for a while. "Yes, I believe they did. Of course Rob was late, but that's to be expected. The whole English department lives in a different world — the nineteenth century, I think."

"I know what you mean," I said. "Although a few of them might still inhabit the sixteenth century, or perhaps an alternate universe altogether. But what about the staff meeting? Would that be just the administrators?"

"Well, yes, Granny and Alan — plus the admissions people."

"And what about Mrs. Archer? Why was Sabena having lunch with her?" I suppressed a smile, thinking of Elaine's characterization of the four Archer girls.

"Hmmmph! We expelled her daughter Marcy last week. I think she was trying to persuade Sabena to take Marcy back. But of course Sabena was adamant." At the mention of Sabena's name, Jane's eyes filled with tears again.

I made some sympathetic noises and forged on. "Punkin and the others are all students, right? What were they seeing Sabena about, do you know?"

"They were all in trouble for one thing or another." She sniffled quietly into her handkerchief. "This was their chance to plead their cases, before they were suspended."

"And were they suspended?"

"Well, if Sabena made any decisions on those girls, she didn't tell me. So you could say the suspensions have been suspended for the time being." Jane smiled again, in spite of herself. "I assume that Alan, as assistant head and dean of students, will make some decisions soon."

I decided not to push my luck. Jane was too distracted to be curious about my interrogating her, but I thought I'd better leave before she became suspicious of my motives. Well, maybe one more question.

"Jane, could it have been a burglary? Was anything missing from the office?"

"You know, the police asked me the same thing. No, there was nothing obvious missing. But maybe it was some little thing. If the police would only let me in there again, maybe I could spot something."

"Perhaps they will. Well, I hope this all settles down soon, for everyone's sake. But now I'm late for John's class. Thanks, Jane."

CHAPTER SEVEN

"The sleek, expensive girls I teach,
Younger and pinker every year,
Bloom gradually out of reach."
William DeWitt Snodgrass, *April Inventory*

"If a man can't live on a dollar a day, then what is he?"
boomed John deHavilland.

His teddy-bear body seemed to grow taller as he spoke, and
his eyes glared maniacally from behind his owlish glasses. John
was doing his impersonation of Henry Ward Beecher, much
to the delight of his American History class. As he ranted on
about the deserving and the undeserving poor, I looked at the
faces of the girls who filled the room. A few were smiling, but
most of them were open-mouthed, awestruck at the nineteenth
century preacher who had suddenly materialized before them.

Nini Westmore, whom I'd met outside Jane Ackerman's
office, was in the class, along with her slime-dating friend Mandy.
They maintained their sophisticated senior status by looking
only mildly amused at John's performance. I recognized two
other girls in the class from their starring roles in Elaine's most
recent production — Shauna Thompson and Tiffany Wood —
both on Sabena's calendar on the fateful day. They were caught
up in the magic of John's drama. Tiffany was beautiful in a way
that I'd come to associate with Wintonbury — tall and slim,
with shoulder-length black hair, pale but perfect skin, and startling blue eyes that now gazed adoringly at her teacher. A junior,
she could still allow herself to express enthusiasm for her classes.

Shauna Thompson was stunning too, in many ways a more commanding presence than Tiffany. One of two African-American girls in the class, she was almost six feet tall, broad-shouldered and athletic-looking. Her flashing brown eyes seemed to take the world in at a glance and judge it as not quite worthy of her. But John deHavilland was a heroic exception, and she gave him her rapt attention.

I hoped to be able to talk to Tiffany and Shauna after class, so I watched the clock impatiently despite the energy of the class I was observing. When John finally dismissed the class, I yelled, "See you at lunch!" to my old friend and ran to catch up with the two girls who were hurrying across campus to their next class.

"Shauna, Tiffany! Can I grab you for a moment or two?"

"Dr. Lombardi, hi. How'd you like the class?" asked Shauna.

"Isn't Mr. deHavilland, you know, amazing?" asked Tiffany almost simultaneously.

"He is wonderful," I agreed. "And I saw a lot of student participation patterns that I can use in my research. But can I ask you something that has nothing to do with your class or Mr. deHavilland?"

"Sure, I guess so," Shauna replied, looking down at me a bit warily.

"You were both on Dr. Lazlo's appointment schedule on Monday. What did you have to see her about? Would you mind telling me?"

They exchanged looks. Tiffany sighed.

"Oh, it was so dumb. We were both a little drunk coming back from the Stratford Hall dance, and Mrs. Lyons — she's our dorm parent — caught us. So we had to, you know, go see Dr. Lazlo about why we shouldn't be suspended."

"But she wasn't going to suspend you, Tiffany! It was your first offense. Now, *me*, I'd been caught before, so I was in bigger trouble."

"And did she suspend you, Shauna?" I asked.

"Nope," she said with a proud grin. "I talked her out of it. She wasn't as tough as she made out to be."

"And tell me about the night she died."

"Oh God," said Tiffany. "Wasn't that awful? My mom wants me to come home. She thinks this place isn't safe any more."

"You mean, where were we when she died?" Shauna asked, immediately getting to the heart of the matter. "Are we, like, suspects or something?"

"No, of course not. I'm just asking people questions."

"Are you working for the police?" Tiffany was wide-eyed.

"No, just trying to satisfy my own curiosity."

"Well, we've all asked ourselves where we were when the Empress was shot," said Shauna. "It was pretty late at night, they're saying, so everyone was in their dorms. I know I was staying up working on an English paper."

"But we didn't hear anything!" added Tiffany emphatically.

"We've all asked ourselves that too, and so did the police."

"Could someone be out of her dorm after hours without anyone knowing?" I asked. A furtive look passed between them.

"Well, sure, we're not locked in, you know," answered Shauna.

"But *we'd* never sneak out!" Tiffany put in at once. She looked again at Shauna.

"Hey, we're late for class now. Gotta go." Shauna grabbed Tiffany's arm and pulled her away.

"Bye!" yelled Tiffany over her shoulder.

Were they protecting each other, I wondered, or someone else? I walked quickly back to the administration building where I would join John for lunch before returning to the university. Jane was standing at the door to Sabena's office. The yellow tape was gone.

"The police have finally let me in," she sighed, "and I've spent the last hour searching to see if anything's missing."

"Is anything?"

"Well, this is so silly, but yes, I think something is. I guess I should tell the police, but it seems so trivial."

"What is it?" I couldn't stand it any longer.

"It's her *Bartlett's Quotations*. Sabena always kept that book on the right-hand corner of her desk, and it isn't there anymore!"

CHAPTER EIGHT

"Suspicion always haunts the guilty mind."
William Shakespeare, *King Henry the Sixth, Part III*

John deHavilland let out a whoop of laughter when I told him the news, the first time I'd seen him really laugh since Sabena's murder. Seniors at the next table turned and gave us curious looks. The dining room had been uncharacteristically subdued until that moment, a reflection of the school's sense of loss.

"Shh," I said to John.

"But it's so funny!"

"I know, I know. Imagine Sabena without her *Bartlett's*." I chuckled in spite of my resolve to look solemn.

"Imagine Wintonbury without Sabena," he replied. "That's even better."

"It's that kind of talk that's gotten you elected prime suspect," I reminded him. "I can't believe that you can talk like that."

"There's a lot you wouldn't believe, Susan. You have no idea how bad it's been around here the last few years. After all, you jumped ship."

"John, don't start that again, please. It was time for me to move on, that's all."

"But how I wish you were still here. Remember all the fun we used to have? Doing crossword puzzles in the Faculty Room? How the seniors used to hang out over the faculty coffeepot and chitchat?"

"Of course, I remember. I was one of the loyal denizens of the Faculty Room, just like you."

"Well, none of that goes on anymore. The Faculty Room is for faculty only, and no one hangs out there much. We all just huddle in our classrooms. We've lost our sense of community." John looked melancholy as we began to clear our dishes from the corner table at which we had sequestered ourselves at lunch.

"I know," I said. "The community started to fall apart almost as soon as Sabena arrived. But maybe with Granny and Alan at the helm, things can go back to the way they once were. You can just be one happy, if eccentric, family again."

"Probably not too happy till the police find Sabena's murderer," he replied.

"Everyone seems convinced that it was someone here, John, but I'm not so sure. What do you know about Sabena's past before she came to Wintonbury? You were on the search committee that brought her here, right?"

"That was over eight years ago. I don't remember a lot. It was a good résumé."

"Eight years ago, hmm. Would Jane still have that résumé in her files? I wonder ...."

"I've got to get to class now," said John, giving me a peck on the cheek. "Guess you professors get more than twenty minutes for lunch, huh?"

We put our dishes on the conveyor belt and headed our separate ways, John back to Manderson Hall and I back to Jane's office. Jane wasn't back from her lunch yet, the policeman had left, and no one seemed to be around.

I hesitated for a while at the door of her office, then slowly sauntered in. Behind Jane's puritanically neat desk were a pair of filing cabinets. The top drawer of the right-hand cabinet was labeled *Personnel* in Jane's precise handwriting.

I looked quickly back over my shoulder — still no Jane. I pulled the drawer open, and my fingers went quickly to the letter *L*. There was a file marked *Lazlo*. Where was Jane? Why was she exposing me to this temptation?

The first thing in the Lazlo file was her résumé. In fact, there were several copies of it. No one would miss one, I reasoned as I pulled one out and jammed it into my briefcase. Then I quickly returned to my place at the door of the office. A minute later, Jane appeared.

"Jane," I said, trying to sound nonchalant. "I just wanted to say good-bye for now. I'll be back for some more observations later in the week. I hope things return to normal soon."

"Good-bye, Susan. We all miss you. Thank you for your good wishes."

I was still flushed with guilt when I climbed into my car to go to Metropolitan.

CHAPTER NINE

"We are the people of this generation, bred in at
least modest comfort, housed now in universities,
looking uncomfortably to the world we inherit."
Students for a Democratic Society,
Port Huron Statement, 1962, Preamble

I pulled into a parking space at the university and mused
glumly over the contrast between the varied architectural splen-
dors of Wintonbury and the box-like, cinder block monotony
of Metropolitan. Something to mention in my next lecture on
social class and education, I thought, making a mental note as
I hurried to my office. I was eager to spend some time studying
Sabena's résumé.

But it was not to be. I had no sooner settled into my desk
chair when Nanette Lehman, the chair of my department, came
to my office.

"We've got trouble," she said, dismay shadowing her usually
friendly face. "The art department is staging a coup."

"What's going on?" I asked.

"Seems they want to remove all the education courses from
their art education program."

"What? Can they do that?"

She leaned her tall, thin body against the doorjamb and
sighed loudly. "Well, a department can propose any program it
likes, of course. But then it has to get passed by subcommit-
tees and the university-wide committee, and confirmed by the
Faculty Senate."

"And how do I figure into this process?"

"As our Curriculum Committee rep, it's your job to forestall this," she explained. "Meet with their chair and see if you can get this proposal withdrawn. Otherwise, things could get ugly at the committee meeting."

"Yipes, Nanette! I've never done this sort of thing. I...."

"Time to learn about campus politics, Susan. Call the chair and make an appointment to see him — before the Curriculum Committee meets."

The committee was scheduled to meet in a little over two weeks.

"Okay, Nanette, I'll get right on it." So much for Sabena's résumé. I found the phone directory amid the clutter of my desk and looked up the art department. The chairman's name was Scott Jeffries. I had never met him.

I punched in his number and got his secretary, who put me right through.

"Dr. Jeffries? It's Susan Lombardi. I'm in secondary education. I need to talk to you about your Curriculum Committee proposal."

I heard him chuckle. "I knew I'd be hearing from one of you ed folks soon. Sure, I'd be glad to talk to you. How's tomorrow morning? Say at ten-thirty?"

"That's fine, thanks. I'll come to your office then."

Well, that was easy enough, I thought. Now for the résumé. But there was a student waiting to see me.

"Dr. Lombardi, I need to get into your class," she whined.

With a resigned sigh, I put the résumé back in my briefcase.

* * *

It was four P.M. and growing dark outside. I had spent the entire afternoon dealing with students whose very lives seemed to depend on getting into classes that were oversubscribed or for which they didn't have the prerequisites. Classes had begun already, but that didn't stop the persistent ones from trying. This last young man was sitting there, leaning forward, eagerly trying to persuade me to admit him to my already full class.

"But if I don't take this course this semester, I won't have the prerequisite for the course I need next fall. And then I won't be able ...."

I looked into his big, brown eyes. He was so sincere. How could I say no? What difference would one more student make? (I tried to repress the memory of the other five students I had already admitted into the course today.) Besides, this was the easiest way to get rid of him. I signed the admission slip.

"Thanks a lot, Dr. Lombardi! I'll work hard. You'll be glad you let me into your class."

"I'm sure I will, Vito. See you on Monday." I locked the door behind him.

I got out the résumé and stared at it. It looked like the résumé of any academic in the world of prep schools — degrees, teaching experience, administrative positions. Was there anything there the least bit suspicious? If so, I couldn't spot it.

I thought about my conversation with John deHavilland earlier in the day. He had called it a "good résumé" — whatever that meant. I knew that at four o'clock I could find John at home. A single parent, he would always be there when his ten-year-old son Jason got home from school, even if his headmistress had been murdered and he was the number one suspect.

Sure enough, his booming voice answered the phone on the first ring.

"John, it's Susan. How's it going?"

"How's it going? Well, let's see. I've been interviewed by the police, again. My colleagues are still avoiding me, my students are hysterical, and now I get a call from an old friend who deserted me five years ago."

"John, please stop harping on that. I need your help. I've got Sabena's résumé here in front of me and I...."

"You've got *what?*" he bellowed.

"Shh," I said unreasonably. Since John was home, it really didn't matter what he said or how loudly, unless Jason was standing right there.

"Susan, what are you doing with Sabena's résumé?"

"I, uh, kind of lifted it from Jane's files." I paused for a moment to let John get his laughing over with.

"Okay, Miss Marple, or is it Kinsey Milhone? What do you want me to tell you?"

"You said that the search committee thought it was a good résumé, right? But was there anything on it that was at all questionable? Or suspicious?" I really didn't have any idea what I was hoping to find.

"Of course not. We read it over, thought it looked impressive, made a few phone calls to schools where she had worked. Then we called her in for an interview. We were as thorough as any search committee ever is."

"But what if some of it is a lie?"

"Susan, what are you hoping to uncover?"

I sighed. "I guess I'm looking for something — anything — that would take the suspicion off you and the others at Wintonbury."

"That's sweet, Susan, and I appreciate your trying. But I guess people like us just have to leave these things to the professionals."

Where had I heard that before? "Okay, thanks, John. Give Jason a big hug for me. Give yourself one too."

"Hugs to you too, Susan. Don't worry about us. Go get some work done."

I hung up the phone. Behind his usual bravado, I could hear the fear. He was so alone — his wife had left years ago to find herself and was now somewhere in Montana living on a ranch. John had no real friends left on the Wintonbury faculty either. One by one, they had left in the years since Sabena had become headmistress.

But John had stayed, largely because of Jason. Raising him in the Wintonbury community made it much easier being a single parent, and of course the house that the school provided for them was larger and cozier than anything John could afford on his own. I knew his sense of feeling trapped was one of the reasons that John had resented my leaving the school.

What could I do for him now? I wasn't much of an amateur sleuth: I was still feeling guilty about snooping in Jane's files. I certainly didn't know the first thing about criminal investigation. Did I know anyone who could help?

And then a name came into my head: Mark Goldin. Or rather Mark Goldin, Private Investigator, though I'd never thought of him that way before.

To explain who Mark Goldin is, I have to describe what I do at Metropolitan University. What I do is teach teachers — would-be teachers, that is. And many of the students at Metropolitan who want to be teachers have led previous lives as something else. Some are mothers who are returning to school after raising families. Some are laid-off engineers. Others have been journalists, business people, drill sergeants, and just about anything you could think of. But Mark Goldin was special. Mark had had more careers than anyone I'd ever met.

Born five years earlier or ten years later, Mark probably would have graduated from Rutgers University and become the doctor or dentist that his nice Jewish mother in New Jersey had envisioned. Instead, he entered Rutgers in the late 1960s, discovered drugs and student protests, and broke his mother's heart by flunking out. Not long afterwards, Mark found himself aboard a ship stationed off the coast of Vietnam. Since then, he had been a truck driver, a computer programmer, a restaurant manager, a building contractor, and a steeplejack.

When he finally decided to try college again in his early forties, Mark did brilliantly. But much to Mama Goldin's dismay, he enrolled at the University of New Haven, majored in criminal justice, and got a license as a private investigator. A few years of PI work for the insurance companies in Hartford convinced him that what he really wanted to do was teach history. And that's how he ended up as a student at Metropolitan University and in two of my classes.

Recognizing how bright he was, I'd used him as an assistant on several research projects. We'd become friends through working together, but I'd never thought I'd need his expertise as an investigator until now. Please be home, Mark, I thought as I punched in his home phone number.

"Mark," I said when he'd picked up the phone. "Did you hear about the murder at Wintonbury?"

"Susan?" I'd forgotten to identify myself.

"Yes, it's Susan. So have you heard about the murder?"

"Yes, I heard about it." He paused. "Do you know anything that the public-at-large doesn't?"

"No, I wish I did." I sighed loudly into the phone.

"Then why are you calling me?" He sounded impatient; maybe I'd interrupted a late afternoon nap. He must have regretted his grumpiness because he quickly added, "Not that I don't enjoy hearing from you anytime."

"Remember my friend John deHavilland? He thinks the police consider him a suspect. I thought you might be able to help him."

"I've worked on insurance fraud cases, Susan, not murders."

"But you took the criminalistics courses, you've got the license! Isn't there anything you can do?"

"Well, I...."

"Look Mark, can you come to my office tomorrow some time in the morning? I've got office hours from nine till noon."

"I do have a class at ten. Maybe I could come by before that. Nine-fifteen? But really, I don't think...."

"See you then! Thanks so much, Mark. I knew I could count on you!"

I closed up my office and went home. As I came in the door, Swash called, "I'm downstairs!"

I hurried down to his office to kiss him hello.

Looking up from his computer, Swash grinned at me. "And what has the little sleuth been up to today?"

Is it possible for a husband to know his wife too well?

CHAPTER TEN

"I have had playmates, I have had companions,
In my days of childhood, in my joyful school days—
All, all are gone, the old familiar faces."
Charles Lamb,
Old Familiar Faces

"Okay," said Mark, settling his long, thin frame into a chair. "Tell me more about Wintonbury Academy. It's a school for spoiled rich girls, right?"

"Now, Mark, I expect more from you. You know that schools like Wintonbury take a considerable number of kids on scholarship. They're not *all* spoiled and rich!" I knew that he was purposely needling me, but I couldn't help defending the school that I had loved.

And Mark couldn't help grinning at my fervor. "Now that you've made that clear...."

"Now that I've made that clear," I repeated, "what is it that you want to know?"

"Tell me all you can about the people there. Your former colleagues."

I paused a moment to think about where to begin. "Let me start with Sabena, herself. She descended on Wintonbury eight years ago, and there's no one left who has a good word to say about her. We were all so excited when the search committee found her — the whole faculty was won over by her when she came for her first interview. She spoke eloquently about having respect for our autonomy as teachers and admiring our professionalism. But within a year, we realized that all Sabena really cared about was glorifying the name of Sabena Lazlo."

"Where did she come from?"

"She had been academic dean at a similar school in Florida, and naturally they gave her ecstatic recommendations. Of course, what they were really ecstatic about was getting rid of her."

"What was she like?"

"Hmm, tall, slim, dark, very chic. Late forties. A little trace of an accent. We thought it was Eastern European, maybe, but no one ever dared to ask, and she never mentioned her origins. She was totally absorbed in her present glory as headmistress of the elite Wintonbury Academy. She loved hobnobbing with the rich parents and alumnae. Faculty were merely the hired hands. And heaven help you if you disagreed with her."

"I take it you disagreed with her on more than one occasion?" Mark asked, looking amused.

"On many occasions. And each time, it became clear that I had earned another demerit in her eyes. Finally I couldn't take the stress of working at a school that was so clearly heading in all the wrong directions. All the joy was gone, so I left."

"And the people who stayed? Would any of them really want to kill her?"

I thought about this for a long while. "Well, nobody liked her. But hating someone enough to kill her is a different story, isn't it?"

Mark shrugged. "Someone did. Who are some of the other people in the top administrative positions? They are the ones she probably had the most contact with."

"Let's see. There's Granny Smith."

"Not her real name, I presume?"

"Of course not. It's Margaret Smith, but she's been there so long and just seems to be everyone's grandma. She's the assistant dean of faculty. A widow with grown children."

"The least likely suspect?" Mark's gray eyes narrowed with interest.

"Well, I wouldn't say that, necessarily. She was very hurt about being overlooked when Sabena started searching for a new dean of faculty. Granny's devoted her life to Wintonbury, and as assistant dean, she probably should have gotten the job. But of course, Sabena was looking for someone younger and more dynamic."

"What happened to the old dean of faculty?"

"Oh, that was Ralph McLaren. He retired to Arizona last year. Probably saw the handwriting on the wall. You don't think he came back and killed her, do you?"

"I don't think anything yet," he said. "Who else is there besides Granny?"

"Well, there's Alan Lyons. He's the assistant head of the school and dean of students. He's late thirtyish, tall and blond, athletic, a Norse god. Married with two kids. Sabena hired him. There was a rumor that they were having an affair."

"Aha! Sex enters the picture at last." He leaned forward intently. "How likely is it that the rumor was true?"

"Mark, I just don't know. In small schools like Wintonbury, rumors fly around all the time. Exchanging gossip keeps the students entertained on long winter nights. And when there aren't any current rumors, they invent them. Faculty affairs — real or imagined — are a favorite topic. But I did notice that he was keeping a low profile at the special assembly about Sabena. Maybe that's significant."

"Okay, let's see if I've got the administrators straight. Sabena, headmistress and egotist, now deceased. Granny Smith, assistant dean of faculty and everyone's favorite sweet old lady. Dean of faculty position currently vacant. Ralph McLaren, retired. Alan Lyons, dean of students, assistant head of the school and possible paramour. Anyone I've left out?"

"I'd say you summed that up very well."

"How about the rest of the faculty? Does anyone come to mind as a likely candidate for a murderer?"

I pictured the faces of many dear friends and former colleagues. "Mark, I worked with those people for years! None of them ever seemed to be homicidally inclined to me. I can tell you one thing, though. My friend John didn't do it! He's a vegetarian — too kind-hearted to eat meat. But the police think he's the chief suspect. Now what can you do to help?"

Mark scratched his salt-and-pepper beard thoughtfully. "Actually, Susan, not much. With my private investigator's license, I can do a surveillance. I can advertise my services. Other than that, you can do as much as I can. Probably more, since you know the people and the way the school works."

"But you must be able to help somehow. Do you have any friends on the Wintonbury police force who maybe could tell you something? Something that's not in the papers yet?"

"I do have one friend. We went through the University of New Haven together. Remember I told you about my lab partner in the forensic science course?"

"Yes, I vaguely remember your story about him. Didn't the two of you spill a corrosive chemical on some evidence you were supposed to be testing?"

"Yeah, he's the one. I still shudder at the memory of that. I doubt he'll be able to give me much. I'll try, though."

"Good. And here's a copy of Sabena's résumé. See if you can find anything interesting in that. Now what next?"

"Are they letting outsiders on their campus right now?"

"Outsiders? Probably not. I know they're keeping the press away. But I'm not an outsider, remember? I'll be back there in a day or two. What should I do?"

"You should go there and talk to some of your old colleagues. Talk to some students too. Meanwhile, I'll try my friend in the police department." He stood up to go. "Got to get to class now."

I stood too. "Mark, John won't be able to afford to pay you."

"I'm not doing this for John. I'm doing this for the fun of working with you again." He grinned, his gray eyes laughing.

It was a very unprofessional thing to do right there in my office, but I gave Mark a big hug and a kiss on the cheek.

I think he was blushing underneath his beard as he left.

CHAPTER ELEVEN

"A patronizing disposition always has
its meaner side."
George Eliot, *Adam Bede*

Scott Jeffries sat behind a massive wooden desk in one of the largest faculty offices I had ever seen on Metropolitan's campus. I did some quick mental measurements. He could have fit four offices like mine in there, with room left over for bookshelves. He was dressed in jacket and tie, very formal for our university. With a full head of white hair and a prominent forehead, he was quite a handsome man.

"So you are Susan Lombardi," he began. "I've heard good things about you from our students."

"Thank you," I said, giving him what I hoped was a gracious smile.

"But I didn't expect anyone quite so young and lovely."

I wasn't sure I liked the tone of that. I took the chair on the other side of his desk and leaned towards him. "Listen, Dr. Jeffries, if your students think so much of me, why are you trying to cut my courses from your art education program?"

"Oh, all business, are you? Too bad. I thought we might get to know each other a bit first."

"Uh, well, I ...."

"How long have you been here, Dr. Lombardi?" he asked, smiling again.

"Five years. It's been...."

"I've been here for almost thirty years," he interrupted. "I've been chair of this department for twelve of those years."

"Thirty years? Twelve as chair? That's...."

"And I know how things work around here." He pounded his desk for emphasis.

"I'm sure you do," I conceded. "But can we talk about your proposal? Why are you asking to drop the education courses from your program?"

"Well, Susan, it's like this." I wondered when had we gotten to a first-name basis. "We are trying to get accredited by the National Art Education Association. In order to do that, we need to increase the number of art courses our students take. We also need to add several art history courses. There just isn't room in their programs for the education courses."

If he could use first names, so could I. "But Scott, it is an art *education* program, isn't it?"

"Well, yes, but we figure that we can just stick some educational jargon into our art classes and...."

"Jargon?" It was my turn to interrupt. "Is that what you think we teach your — our — students?"

"Now, I'm sure you teach them some very nice things, Susan. But they can pick that sort of stuff up on their own during their student teaching. Meanwhile, we need to get this accreditation." He leaned back in his chair and folded his arms across his chest.

"Scott, we teach them important skills they need before they start their student teaching! I'm really concerned that your students will be terribly lost without our courses. Let's look at those accreditation requirements together. Perhaps we can find some other courses that can be cut."

"Why certainly, Susan. I'll have my secretary make you a copy of the accreditation requirements, and then when you've had a chance to study them, we can get back together." He rose from his chair and walked towards the door, indicating that the meeting was over.

"I'll look at them tonight," I said, walking with him out the door. "Let's meet again tomorrow morning. Ten o'clock?" I desperately wanted to get this worked out before the subcommittee meeting.

"I'll look forward to it," he replied with an ingratiating smile.

I went back to my office, which felt like a cubbyhole after the spaciousness of Jeffries's domain. My cheeks were burning with fury.

I looked up a few moments later to find Nanette Lehman standing outside my office door.

"Nanette, that was awful! He thinks that all we teach in our courses is a bunch of jargon."

"I'm sure many of our Arts and Sciences colleagues would agree with him, Susan," she replied.

"But that's so unfair! And he gives me the creeps. He's so patronizing."

"Yes, I know. Handsome and arrogant, just the way I like them, unfortunately." She gave me a wry smile. "How did you leave things with him?"

"I've got a copy of the accreditation requirements for the National Art Education Association right here. According to Jeffries, they have to drop our courses in order to meet these requirements. But I can't believe that."

"Neither can I," she agreed. "Take a close look at them tonight and compare them to what we're requiring right now. See if we have any leeway. I've already alerted the dean that a battle may be imminent."

"Oh, I hope not. Maybe we can find some compromise."

"I hope you're right. Things can get ugly around here when turf battles start up. You may need to get some testosterone injections."

CHAPTER TWELVE

"A professor can never better distinguish himself in his work than by encouraging a clever pupil, for the true discoverers are among them, as comets amongst the stars."
Benjamin Daydon Jones,
Biography of Linnaeus

"Susan," Mark began. "I was afraid you might have gone out to lunch. I just had to tell you, I've just had another one of those incredible classes...."

"Like the lecture Benedetto gave on why teachers shouldn't lecture?"

"Sort of. But this was Dr. Smythe. She was giving a lecture on stress and time management, but she never got to the time management part because she ran out of time."

I groaned. "Well, my morning hasn't been much more rewarding than yours. But I just remembered that I forgot to tell you one thing earlier. Something was stolen from Sabena's office."

"Something important?"

"Well, something very funny actually. John and I were falling over in hysterics at lunch yesterday." Mark was drumming his fingers impatiently as I giggled. "I guess you'd like to know what it is. Her *Bartlett's Quotations* is gone!"

"And why is that so uproariously amusing?"

"Oh God, you'd have to have worked for Sabena to get the joke. Every week at the school assembly, she gave a speech to students and faculty, and she always started it with a quotation. When she spoke to parents, she always started with a quotation.

When she spoke to alumnae, she always started with a quotation. We used to joke that if someone would only steal her *Bartlett's*, she'd be speechless!"

"And now someone has. But if someone wanted to stop her incessant quoting, he — or she — could have just taken her book. On the other hand, if you're going to kill her, why steal the book? Doing both doesn't make sense."

I stopped laughing. "Mark, you're right. John and I were so carried away with the humor of it all that I never thought about that. Unless there was something in the book that someone wanted."

"Are you sure the book is really gone?" He looked at me skeptically.

"Jane swears she searched Sabena's office thoroughly, and Jane is *very* thorough. She also got the key to Sabena's house on campus and searched there too."

"Well, I'm not convinced that the missing *Bartlett's* is related to the murder. But I did look over the résumé and couldn't find anything questionable. What can you personally verify?" He took out a pen and started making notes in a notebook. I noticed that the notebook was supposed to be for Dr. Smythe's course. Mark had obviously decided that he would not be taking a lot of notes in her class.

"We know from my e-mail that she *was* at Tamarac. Let's see, what else do I know for sure? She was at Marston School. We know that from Jack Lonnigan's email, and he seems to confirm her MA from Pennsylvania."

"Wouldn't the Wintonbury board have checked up on this anyway?"

"They certainly would have called Tamarac about her, maybe the other schools in her employment history. If Tamarac had spoken glowingly about her, I don't know that they would have checked up on all her degrees."

"Why not?"

"Each school that hired her probably checked with the school she was at previously. Some schools do ask for transcripts from graduate schools though. So you think she lied about her degrees?"

"People have been known to do that. But what could this possibly have to do with her murder?"

"I just keep thinking that there's something in her past that led to her murder."

Mark gave me a stern look. "You just don't want to believe that someone at Wintonbury could be capable of murder."

"Maybe," I admitted. "But I think something else may have happened that night that the students know about and aren't telling." I explained about the furtive looks that Tiffany and Shauna had exchanged during my conversation with them.

"Hmm, you need to talk to those girls more. For now, let's try to reconstruct Sabena's life. Are there are any years missing on this résumé? It's always suspicious when there are years unaccounted for."

"Okay. B.A., Barnard College, 1971. So presumably she was in New York City from 1967 to 1971."

"*Unless* she took more than four years, of course."

"Yes," I said. "We know some very fine people who took more than four years to get their bachelor's."

"Mm-hmm," Mark agreed with a deprecating grin.

"Then," I continued, "we have her at University of Pennsylvania from 1971 to 1973, getting her master's degree."

"Could she have done that in only one year? Then we would have a year unaccounted for."

"Maybe. Let's keep that possibility in mind." I made a note of that. "Okay, now we go to the employment history. Here, she's at Marston School in Manhattan from 1973 through 1978."

"And she got her doctorate from Columbia in 1979, so she must have been teaching and taking courses at the same time for a while. That must have been a hefty load to carry. But it doesn't leave too much time unaccounted for, does it?" He looked with disappointment at the résumé.

"But again, there might be some time that she was somewhere else besides UPenn or Columbia that's not listed here. We really need to know the exact dates she attended Barnard, UPenn, and Columbia. Those dates of attendance aren't on her résumé."

"Well, perhaps we can get them," Mark said. "What about after her doctorate?"

"That takes us back to her employment history. Here it is, Rolling Hills Academy in Virginia from 1979 to 1984, then Tamarac from 1984 to 1992. And in 1992, heaven help us all, she descended upon Wintonbury."

"So aside from some questions about how many years she took to get each degree, we really can't find anything at all questionable."

"There must be something."

"Susan," he interrupted. "Don't you have a one o'clock class to teach?"

"Oops! Do I teach here? I forget that sometimes. Meet me back here in an hour?"

CHAPTER THIRTEEN

"I do not mind lying, but I hate inaccuracy."
Samuel Butler, *Notebooks*

"So then, cognitive theory, or at least Ausubel's theory, says we should always start a lesson with the Big Idea?" asked Vito earnestly.

"I think that sums it up very well," I said, eager to end the class and get back to my office. Vito beamed at me. Yes, I was glad I had admitted him to my class, just as he had promised.

"So for our lesson plans this week, we have to come up with a Big Idea?" asked another student.

"Yes, that's a good way to look at it," I agreed, keeping my impatience in check.

"But what if there is no Big Idea in the subject matter we're teaching?" whined one young woman.

Why is it that every class has a whiner? Whether they are the elite students of Wintonbury Academy or the decidedly middle-class students at Metropolitan, there is always at least one per class.

"Then ask yourself why you're teaching it," I responded. "What is the most important thing that you want your students to come away with from the class? Remember Sizer's idea about the essential questions of your discipline? Go back to that."

She looked at me dubiously. I answered some more students' questions about the next assignment and then hurried back to my office. Mark was still there, slouching in a chair and staring down at a framed photograph in his hand. It was a photo of Swash, Joanne, and me taken the previous summer in the Colorado Rockies.

"Nice picture," he said, putting it back on my desk.

"Thanks. We had a terrific time throwing snowballs in July there." I did some rearranging of the papers on the desk to make room for the books I was carrying. "Any beeps on my computer?"

"A few. I didn't think I should read your e-mail though."

"Well, let's see if there's anything back from Jeannette Richardson or Jack Lonnigan or Kathy What's-her-name."

Sure enough, Jeannette Richardson had replied:

Dear Susan:

Sabena's résumé said she had graduated from Barnard College in 1971. My sister also was Barnard Class of '71, so I asked her about Sabena. She had never heard of her, which wasn't that surprising. But when she checked her old yearbook and her commencement program, there was no Sabena Lazlo there either. Of course, maybe Sabena just had the year wrong on her résumé, but don't you think one would be careful about that? I think she was lying about having been at Barnard, for some reason. I never followed up on it though. I hope this helps.

Jeannette Richardson

"Wow! I can't believe that. Why would Sabena lie about the college she went to? Or the year she graduated?" Secretly, I was delighted at the thought of Sabena's having lied about her academic accomplishments. She had been so pretentious about her prestigious alma maters.

"Of course, Susan, you realize that you are getting this third-hand from Jeannette Richardson's sister."

"Yes, but it's definitely worth looking into, don't you think? Mark, do you have any classes tomorrow?"

He looked at me uncertainly. "No, but I was hoping to get an early start on my paper for Radinsky's class."

"Couldn't you go to New York tomorrow morning and start your paper tomorrow afternoon?" I felt a little pang of guilt asking this of a student, I must confess.

"New York? Oh, you mean go to Barnard and find out if there ever was a Sabena Lazlo there?"

"Yes. They probably have old yearbooks in the library and maybe there are class lists or commencement programs in the archives. Maybe there's an alumnae directory."

"That's a lot of maybes." Mark was still dubious. "And there's a little matter that, uh ...." His voice trailed off.

"Travel expenses will be provided," I reassured him. Swash was going to love this!

"Okay, so I should go to Barnard and see what I can find out about Sabena."

"I wish I could go with you, but I have an appointment tomorrow morning and more work to do at Wintonbury in the afternoon."

"No problem. I'm the PI here, remember?"

"Right. Give me a call from New York tomorrow around noon, will you? I'll be in my office having lunch."

"Check. Will do."

"Speaking of being a PI, have you found anything out from your friend in the Wintonbury police?"

"That's Caz Czaikowski. No, he hasn't been able to give me anything. It's an active case, and he's not supposed to discuss it with anyone. But I'm hopeful that I can still wheedle some information out of him."

"Mark," I said, "you are being wonderful about this."

"Anything for my favorite professor," he replied. "I'll call you."

"Great, thanks," I said, expecting him to leave and surprised when he just stood there. "Thanks, Mark," I repeated. "I thank you. John deHavilland thanks you. Swash thanks you."

I wasn't so sure about that last bit of gratitude.

CHAPTER FOURTEEN

"The present in New York is so powerful that the past is lost."
John Jay Chapman, *Letter, 1909*

In fact, I conveniently forgot to even mention Mark's quest in New York to Swash that night. But I did speak to him about my determination to devise a good compromise proposal with the art department.

"This is the first important thing I've done for my department as Curriculum Committee rep," I explained. "I want it to go well."

"Thinking about tenure?" he asked.

"Yes," I admitted. "But also just doing a good job for my department. And seeing that the art students have a program that prepares them well."

Swash smiled his approval as I went off to immerse myself in program sheets and NAEA standards for art teachers.

* * *

The next morning, I headed off to Jeffries's office, my briefcase full of syllabi and program sheets.

"Dr. Jeffries," I began as his secretary ushered me into his palatial office.

"Call me Scott," he replied, looking up from his computer.

"Okay, Scott," I said with what I hoped was a cordial, collegial smile. "Now, I went through the NAEA requirements, and I think I've found a way to accomplish what you need."

"Such a clever girl."

"Um, Scott, I haven't been a clever *girl* for a long time now."

"Eh? Oh, yes, of course. How non-PC of me. Well, show me what you've come up with." He pantomimed rolling up his sleeves to get down to business.

"See here? You can double-count this art history course so it's part of the history requirement."

"Hmm. Now why didn't I think of that?" He smiled benevolently at me.

"Then you can use the ed psych course to meet the psych requirement and...."

"Yes, yes, I see. I think that works. Yes, very good."

He seemed to be very conciliatory this morning. I wondered if he were really paying attention. Was there something else on his mind?

"Scott," I said. "Do you think the committee will accept all this?"

"I'm sure they will. Now what's this you've done with the computer requirement?"

Satisfied that he had been listening, I explained my idea for incorporating the technology requirement into an art education course. "I think that meets your needs as far as the NAEA goes," I said.

"That's very good, Susan," he said, rising to his feet. "I like it." Clearly I was being dismissed from the royal presence again.

"So we're all set?" I asked.

"Of course," he replied. "I'm not such an unreasonable ogre, am I?"

"No, of course not. Thank you for being so un-ogre-esque. I'm kind of new at university politics and...."

He patted my shoulder in a fatherly way. "Well, you'll learn, my dear, you'll learn."

* * *

I hurried back to my office and logged on to my e-mail. There still was no word from Kathy Marchand about her ex-husband, and I looked in vain for further recollections from Jack Lonnigan. The phone rang just as I stuffed the last piece of sandwich into my mouth.

"Mmmmf. Dr. Lombardi," I said, swallowing hard.

"Susan, it's Mark. I'm in the Barnard library. I've been through all the Barnard College yearbooks from 1960 to 1980, and there's no Sabena Lazlo in any of them."

"Well, she couldn't be so much older or younger that she wouldn't appear in *any* of those yearbooks. You've covered a twenty-year span. Do you think she chose not to have her photo put in the yearbook?"

"I thought of that. There's a list at the back of those who are in the class but not pictured in the yearbook. Still no Sabena Lazlo."

"I guess that pretty much clinches it. She didn't go there!"

Mark grunted his agreement. "As long as I'm here, I'm going to nose around the college archives and the alumnae office and see if there's anything I'm missing."

"Good idea. Let's see. Columbia did become coed at some point, even though it also maintained Barnard as a separate college. Maybe she graduated from Columbia and not Barnard? Can you check that out?"

"Sure," he replied. "She went to grad school here too, right? Maybe I should check up on that as well."

"Yes, her doctorate's supposedly from Columbia Teachers College. See if you can get that confirmed, as long as you're nearby."

"Okay, I can do that. You know, this is kind of interesting."

"Interesting? This is pretty amazing! Why would Sabena lie about going to Barnard?"

"Mm-hmm," he agreed. "Makes you wonder what else she might have lied about, doesn't it?"

"oh i should worry and fret
death and i will coquette
there's a dance in the old dame yet."
Donald Robert Perry Marquis, *archy and mehitabel*

My head spinning with this news, I gulped my coffee and headed out to Wintonbury. I had made an appointment to see Granny Smith that afternoon. Snow was starting to fall again, so I drove slowly, knowing that my mind was not as focused on my driving as it should be. Fortunately, my car seemed to go on auto-pilot from Metropolitan to Wintonbury, and the roads weren't bad yet. I skidded into the visitors' parking lot and slushed across campus to Granny's office.

Margaret Smith sat in front of a computer, wire-rimmed reading glasses perched at the end of her nose. Fingers flew across the keys, and her lips moved silently as she typed.

"I'll be right with you, Susan," she said, barely looking up. "Just a few more changes to make in these schedules."

I sat down and watched her work. As efficient and dedicated as ever, I thought. Why had Sabena passed her over as dean? Too old? Too smart? Too independent? Too frumpy?

"Now then," she began. "What can I do for you, Susan? Other than say how much we all miss you?"

Sweet old Granny! I gave her an appreciative smile, and decided to be honest with her. "I'm, uh, really concerned about John and the police; how they've targeted him as the suspect,

I mean. I thought I might try to do some investigating of my own. Interviewing people about Sabena's...."

"But don't you think that's best left to the police?" she interrupted.

"Well, it's just that I know the place so well and...."

"Surely, you're too busy at the university to get involved with our problems."

Granny could make the CEO of a Fortune 500 company feel like a delinquent student. What a dean she would have been!

"Well, I...."

"And I can't believe that Michael approves of this." Granny Smith was perhaps one of three people in the world who called Swash "Michael." The other two were his mother and his Aunt Rose.

"He doesn't exactly approve but ...."

Granny chuckled. "You always were a bit of a busybody, weren't you, Susan?"

Ouch! Who was interrogating whom here?

"Okay," I admitted. "I am a busybody. And Swash thinks I should be doing my research and thinking about tenure, not murder. And I do have other work to do. But nonetheless, here I am. Won't you indulge my curiosity a bit?"

Her round face beamed at me. "Well, a little indulgence might not hurt. And besides maybe you could actually do us some good. If you find out anything important, will you share it with me? Before you share it with the police?"

"Yes, of course, I will."

"In that case, I'll answer your questions. And I'll encourage the rest of the faculty to do the same. Now, what is it you want to know?"

"Were you on campus when it happened ?"

"No, I was home. I know everyone thinks I never leave this office. I do work late, Susan, but not that late. I'm usually home by eight, snug in my bed reading with Jabber and Wocky by nine." Jabber and Wocky were Granny's two Burmese cats.

"And you heard about the murder when?"

"Not until I arrived at school at seven the next morning to find the police all over the campus and Jane Ackerman sobbing hysterically. Then I did what I could to keep the girls and the faculty calm."

"And do you have any idea who could have killed Sabena?"

Granny brushed a stray cat hair from the lap of her navy wool dress while she thought about my question. "Susan, you know that none of us liked her by now, but can you imagine any of us actually killing her? We're like a family here."

I didn't remind her of the statistics on how often family members kill one another. "But if you had to pick one or two likely suspects?"

Granny wrinkled her nose and readjusted her glasses. "Well, I guess my money would be on John — he did threaten her."

"But he's such a gentle soul," I protested.

"Of course he is. But he was so angry that day. And even the most gentle animal will kill to protect its home and family."

"Anyone else?"

"There's Harry Trout. His job really was on the line this time."

"But he's so...."

"Incompetent? Yes. Nonetheless, he's got a wife to support and two sons in college. And Susan, if you're going to protest every name I bring up, why ask me at all?"

I sighed. "You're right, of course. Anyone else?"

"Well, there's always sweet old Granny Smith, isn't there? She really hated Sabena, you know."

My mouth fell open.

"Now, dear, you mustn't exclude anyone just because you have some affection for them. After all, two Burmese cats don't provide much of an alibi, do they?"

CHAPTER SIXTEEN

"Round up the usual suspects."
Julius Epstein, Philip Epstein & Howard Koch, *Casablanca*

Giving Granny a hug, I headed for Lewis Hall, where English and mathematics classes met. Perhaps I could find Rob Fleming or Harry Trout still in their classrooms. I knew I would be seeing Elaine soon, so I wasn't concerned with finding her.

Classes were just ending, and the girls hurried out of the building. It was Friday afternoon, and they had to catch taxis to the bus station, or watch the afternoon soaps, or primp for dates that evening. A few lingered behind to talk to each other or their teachers.

Harry's classroom was empty. Either he had no last period class or he had let them out early. That would be typical. I looked at the bare walls of his deserted classroom and shuddered.

Rob's classroom was the antithesis of Harry's, decorated with colorful posters of contemporary films with Shakespearean themes. A few girls lingered after senior English, gazing at their idol with adoring eyes. Rob was on the small side but with a classic profile and brooding good looks. He was also a published poet and the only young single man on the Wintonbury faculty (John deHavilland, who was more a father figure than an idol, hardly counted as single).

He looked up and saw me standing in the hallway outside his room.

"Now, my fair flowers," he said to his coterie. "I must be the winter wind and chase you all away." Rob tended to speak in metaphors.

After the girls had reluctantly left, he greeted me warmly. "Susan! Still the bright star in the murky skies of Metropolitan, I suppose?"

"Thanks, Rob, I'm doing fine, yes." The way he talked always reduced me to monosyllables. "But how are you and the school holding up under the strain of Sabena's murder?"

"Ah, the stalwart oak tree e'er resists the winds of scandal."

Wasn't he the wind just a few moments ago? I inadvertently shook my head to clear my brain. One last try.

"Do you have any idea about who might have killed Sabena?"

If I didn't watch out, I would start sounding like Sam Spade — talking to Lord Byron.

"Actually, no." A direct answer! "Sabena was a closed book. There was no way to read her when she was alive, and in death she remains ever more unread." He gazed dramatically up to heaven.

"You went to see her the day she was murdered, didn't you? What was it about?"

"She needed my mental razor to help her cut through the jungle of English department trivia." Rob had recently assumed the chair of the English department. I tried to imagine what it would be like for me to sit through a meeting that he chaired.

The bells from the church across the green brought me out of my reverie. Rob, of course, was still talking about the English department. I looked at my watch. I really should get home, I thought, Swash is waiting.

"Well, nice to see you, Rob. Under the circumstances, you appear to be holding up nicely."

As I headed for my car, I took in great gulps of fresh air. Rob had that effect on me.

Not bad, I thought to myself. I didn't see Harry, and I didn't get anything out of Rob. But I did have Granny's approval to do some snooping. I felt good about that. Investigating a murder wouldn't be very different from doing research, I reassured myself. Just a matter of asking the right questions.

It was Friday afternoon and getting late. Swash and I have a Friday Afternoon Ritual, and I didn't want to disrupt it, so I tried to put the Wintonbury murder out of my head as I drove home through the slushy streets.

Sure enough, Swash was in his blue silk pajamas when I arrived. And he didn't want to talk about Wintonbury.

CHAPTER SEVENTEEN

"I have learned silence from the talkative,
toleration from the intolerant,
and kindness from the unkind; yet strange,
I am ungrateful to those teachers."
Kahlil Gibran, *Sand and Foam*

The following Monday afternoon found me trudging through the snow to keep an appointment with Harry Trout. Harry and his wife Louise lived in a beautiful colonial house on one end of the Wintonbury campus.

Looking tired and mousy as ever, Louise ushered me through the maze of antique furniture into her husband's study. After inquiring whether I would like some tea, she quietly disappeared. I wondered if living with Harry all these years had drained her of all vitality.

"Good to see you, Susan," he said with false heartiness. He didn't bother to rise from his armchair. "To what do I owe this pleasure?"

"As Granny must have explained to you, I'm just talking to faculty about Sabena's death."

He scratched his thinning white hair and took a sip of his tea, avoiding my eyes. "Seems to me that's police work. Why should any of us talk to you about it?"

"Of course, you're right, Harry," I said diplomatically. "But Granny and I thought I might notice something the police missed. I know this place so well after all my years here. I'm also trying to help out John, who seems to be their chief suspect."

Harry snorted at this. "If he's their chief suspect, then there's a good reason for it! We all heard him threaten her!"

And I'll bet you told the police that too, I thought to myself.

He took another sip of tea. I thought I noticed a distinctly alcoholic odor coming from the teacup. "And even if he didn't do it, it serves him right. He's always mouthing off about one thing or another. Thinks he's God's gift to Wintonbury."

"He can be overbearing sometimes," I agreed, hoping to keep him talking. "But you said 'even if he didn't do it.' Is there someone else you suspect?"

"The list of people who wanted to kill Sabena was a mile long. What about Granny? The old biddy has been miffed all year about not getting the dean's job. And then of course, there's a whole student body of potential killers."

"You don't seriously think a student did it, do you, Harry?"

"Well, I'll tell you, Susan, we don't get the kind of students here at Wintonbury that we once did."

"What do you mean?" I asked, although I thought I knew the answer.

"Used to be Wintonbury got only daughters of the finest families. Now we get scholarship students from Harlem and places like that."

I considered dumping his tea over his head but managed to find some self-restraint. An argument over his bigotry wouldn't advance my investigation.

"Maybe Sabena caught one of them in a drug deal," he continued, putting down his cup and folding his hands over his considerable paunch.

"Interesting thought, Harry. Any other suspicions?"

Louise interrupted us as she returned with a cup of tea for me. "Tell her about the thing with Rob Fleming," she prompted him and left the room.

"What about Rob?" I asked.

"Up to his old tricks again. He's sleeping with one of his students. In the old days, a man would lose his job over that, but not anymore."

"Of course, that's just a rumor," I began.

Harry snorted again. "I see her sneaking out of his house in the middle of the night. I can't see her face, but I can see that it's a girl."

"How do you happen to see that in the middle of the night?" I asked.

"I've got insomnia. So I go down to the kitchen to get some warm milk, and I see her. Our kitchen door looks out over the back of Rob's house."

"You weren't up in the middle of the night when Sabena was shot, were you, Harry?"

"Nah. But I've seen the little chippy plenty of other times."

"Why would that make Rob a suspect in the murder? That makes him a lecher maybe, but not a killer."

Another gulp from the teacup. "Sex, drugs, who knows what else the man is up to!"

"Drugs? I thought you said the girls from Harlem were responsible for those." I didn't mean to start an argument, but I couldn't help myself. Fortunately, he missed my sarcasm completely.

"See? There may be a link between them and the goings-on at Fleming's house."

"Oh, yes, I see." I tried not to roll my eyes to the ceiling. "Now about the night of the murder. You say you weren't up that night?"

"Nope, slept like a baby. Just ask Louise. She'll tell you."

"Oh, was *she* up that night?"

"No, why?"

"Then how would she know if you were awake or sleeping?" Gotcha, Harry.

He ignored me. "Besides, why would I bother to kill Sabena?"

I hesitated a moment. "Um, there's a rumor circulating that she was about to fire you."

"Ha! Rumors! Always rumors!" He glared at me and took another gulp of tea. "Well, they don't count for anything. No one's going to fire me from this school. I've outlasted three headmistresses, and I'll outlast three more!"

Not if you keep drinking that "tea," Harry, I thought to myself.

CHAPTER EIGHTEEN

"He knows little who will tell his wife all he knows."
Thomas Fuller, *The Holy State and the Profane State*

Granny had put Alan Lyons as the next person on my schedule to interview. Alan and his family lived in a spacious apartment on the first floor of the newest dormitory on Wintonbury's campus. Having just escaped the heavy atmosphere and Early Americana of Harry Trout's house, I looked forward to the contemporary furnishings and the airiness of the Lyons's home.

Beth and Alan always looked to me as though they should be doing a commercial for a ski resort. Tall, blond, and dressed in casual good taste, they glowed with health and vigor. Alan was an effective administrator and a good teacher, and Beth supervised her dorm with a strong but caring hand, so they were a formidable team.

Beth had their too-perfect baby, Alix, in her arms as she opened the door. But today the baby was fussing and crying, and Beth looked harried.

"Come in, Susan," she said, trying to be gracious while shouting over Alix's howls. "Alan's in the living room. Careful, don't trip on the rollerblades. I keep telling Sean not to leave them at the front door."

"I'll find my way, Beth. You've obviously got your hands full."

She ran her hands through her hair and sighed. "It's been a bad few days," she replied. "Oh, damn, now I've got strained peaches in my hair." She excused herself and hurried off, Alix still squealing in protest.

Alan was sitting on the couch, restlessly flipping channels on the TV with a remote.

"Thanks for seeing me, Alan." I said. "I know you must be incredibly busy running the school."

"Actually, Granny and I are running it together with a lot of help from Jane Ackerman. And I'm sorry that I don't have much time. We've got to be in the school dining room for dinner pretty soon, you know."

"Yes, I remember. Well, I just have a few questions."

"I'm not sure why you're doing this, Susan," he interrupted.

"I, uh, thought that since I know this place so well, and have this friend who's a private detective and all ...." Shouldn't I be getting better at this?

"Yes, Granny seemed to think you might actually be able to help us, so I told her I'd cooperate. But to be honest, I'm dubious."

"I appreciate your honesty," I acknowledged, trying to sound sincere. "Let me just ask you a few questions, okay?"

"Go ahead," he answered, finally hitting the off button on the TV remote.

"First of all, tell me about the administrative staff meeting with Sabena on the day before she was shot. Did anything unusual happen at that meeting?"

"Hmm. Let's see, there was a report from the admissions staff. Nothing unusual there, except that applications are down a bit this year."

"What effect will that have on the school?"

"Not a lot. We'll have to accept a few more students who are weaker academically but can pay the full freight. That's happened before." He smiled grimly. "Of course, this, uh, new development will undoubtedly take its toll on admissions too."

"Well, maybe not too bad a toll if the murder gets solved quickly," I said. "Did anything else happen at the meeting that was out of the ordinary?"

"Oh, yes, of course. There was Sabena's plan to sell off the faculty houses."

"Now who would be affected most by that?"

"Of the people who were at the meeting? None. It won't affect me, because we live in a dormitory. It won't affect Granny or the admissions people because they live off-campus. So it would have been a hardship for only faculty like John deHavilland or Harry Trout, who have those beautiful old houses. I suppose you heard about John's threat to Sabena at the last faculty meeting?"

"Yes," I sighed. "I've heard about it. Again and again. Do you really think he could have killed her?"

Alan returned my sigh. His eyes, normally clear blue and dazzling, were reddened and underlined with dark circles. "I just don't know, Susan. I don't want to think it's anybody at the school."

"Me either. I suppose you were asleep when it happened, like everyone else?"

"Actually, they don't know exactly when it happened, do they? I was up in the middle of that night though, dealing with a dorm problem. Some of the seniors on the third floor were having a histrionic scene about somebody's boyfriend."

"I don't suppose you heard or saw anything suspicious?"

"No, just screaming adolescent girls."

"But that does give you an alibi, sort of, if you need it?"

"If I need it, yes. But I don't need it." He shifted his muscular frame uneasily.

"One last thing, Alan. About the rumors — about you and Sabena?"

He looked at the thick carpet at his feet, lips set tight. "That's irrelevant," he sputtered.

"But not untrue?"

"Think what you like, Susan. It's all over now, in any case. And I do have to get to dinner."

With this he walked me to the door. I shouted a cheery good-bye to Beth, who was somewhere in the apartment getting a loudly complaining Alix dressed to go across campus to the dining room.

I arrived home to a kitchen aromatic with garlic and oregano, and Swash happily stirring a pot of spaghetti sauce. He calls it Swash's Own. It's one more thing he and Paul Newman have in common. I hastily told Swash about my visits to the Trouts and the Lyons.

"So Harry's alibi is pretty weak, and of course, Louise would say anything to cover for him. The old bigot. I wish I really believed he did it."

"But unfortunately, bigotry isn't a crime," Swash said.

"Alan does seem to be under a lot of stress, with all the added responsibilities. Even Beth and Alix were out of sorts."

"Well, that's not too surprising," he said. "With all that's going on there right now, no one is going to be quite normal. You have had a day of husbands and wives, haven't you? And there's some e-mail from two more wives waiting for you."

"Two more wives?"

"Yes, Kathy Marchand has finally returned to her computer, and Jack Lonnigan's wife seems to have remembered something new about Sabena's husband. Susan, where are you going? Damn, I knew I shouldn't have told you until after supper!"

CHAPTER NINETEEN

"'It's a poor sort of memory that only works
backwards,' the Queen remarked."
Lewis Carroll, *Through the Looking Glass*

I raced down the stairs to our office, stepping around the papers from Swash's busy day. Booting up the computer, I read:

Dear Susan,

I'm sorry that I've taken so long to reply to your question. I've been very busy and frankly I didn't want to think about Sabena and what she did to me. But, here's your answer: my husband's name was Richard Westcott and he was getting a doctorate at Columbia Teachers College at the same time that Sabena was. They had an affair, then Rich left me for her. Last I heard (from mutual friends), he was a professor somewhere in Virginia, and their marriage had broken up.
Hope this helps you.
Kathy Marchand

PS. If you ever find Rich, let me know where he is. I still have a few choice words I want to say to him.

Wow! There was the confirmation of husband number two. And the explanation of Sabena's brief sojourn in Virginia. I sent Kathy a short note of thanks, feeling sorry to have made her dredge up those hurtful memories.

But even better news lay ahead:

Dear Susan,

My husband Jack tells me that you are trying to find Sabena's husband. I met him just once at a Christmas party early on in Sabena's years at Marston School. He was sitting all alone in a corner, looking forlorn because Sabena was off flirting with someone else. I felt sorry for him, having a wife like that, so I chatted with him. I don't remember his first name, but his last name was the same as Woody Allen's real name—something-berg. I remember that because when he told me his name, I thought to myself that he looked kind of like Woody Allen. He was from Brooklyn just like Woody Allen too. I remember that I asked him if they were related, but he said no. Jack thought this might be useful to you in finding him.

Nora Lonnigan

"Swash! Hurrah! We've got it!" I called as I came upstairs to dinner. "Sabena did have two husbands! An accountant from Brooklyn named Koenigsberg and a professor named Richard Westcott."

"So she was Sabena Lazlo Koenigsberg Westcott?" he asked. "That's a mouthful."

"Yes, even without all that pasta, that's a mouthful. But she never used those names professionally as far as I can tell. Wow, I can't wait to tell Mark about this. It shouldn't be too hard to trace those two husbands now that we have their names."

I tried to do justice to Swash's Own, but I was too excited to eat very much. Trying not to feel guilty about abandoning Swash, I took my after-dinner coffee to the phone and called Mark.

Mark was equally delighted with the news. "If he's still in the New York City area, it shouldn't be too hard to find the accountant," he said. "Of course there are probably a lot of CPAs named Koenigsberg, but I'll start going through the Yellow Pages and calling them tomorrow."

"Great. That should get us moving again." We had been stymied by what to do next after finding no trace of Sabena as an undergraduate at Barnard or Columbia, although Mark had found confirmation that she had, indeed, gotten her doctorate there.

"How about you doing a search for the Westcott guy, since he's in education?"

"Sure," I agreed. "I can go in early tomorrow and see if he's in *Who's Who in Education*. Maybe I can even search the ERIC database on the computer tonight and see if he's got any articles listed there."

"I think you've got the easier job," Mark chuckled.

"Well, you're the professional," I said. "I am just the bumbling amateur."

"Right, I forgot. Okay, I'll see you in your office tomorrow at four."

I did search the database that night. ERIC is a listing of research papers given at various conferences or published in educational journals. There were lots of Westcotts, but no Richard. The following day, I was disappointed to find that he wasn't listed in *Who's Who* either. The next step was probably to try to get his university affiliation through one of the hundreds of educational organizations, but before I could do that, there were classes to teach and students to help.

And then there was the subcommittee meeting to attend to. I entered the conference room with a light heart, knowing that I had done a good job with Scott Jeffries in finding a compromise that both our departments could live with. As I sat down at the table, Jeffries smiled cordially at me. But then I opened the packets that had been distributed and noticed that the original proposal was still in it.

"Scott," I whispered across the table. "Why is this still here?"

He glanced away quickly. The meeting began, and when we got to Scott's proposal, he did, indeed, present the original one, without a word about our meetings or the compromise plan I thought we had created.

"I am really taken aback by this," I said when it was time for discussion. "Dr. Jeffries and I had discussed a very different program, and I thought we had reached an understanding about that."

Jeffries looked at me and shook his head. "Well, yes, we did, but then when I brought it to my department, they shot it down, so we are proceeding with the original plan."

"And you didn't feel it was necessary to let me know about the change in the proposal before this meeting?" I asked incredulously. I could feel my face flushing with anger.

"I figured you would hear about it here."

"Well, let me just say to this subcommittee what I said to Dr. Jeffries. One, there are several better ways to achieve his goal of getting NAEA accreditation, without cutting any education courses. Two, his students badly need those education courses to enable them to successfully student teach. And three, the state department of education will never approve this program."

"What are some of those better ways?" asked one of the subcommittee members.

I distributed copies of my alternative plan that I had brought along in my briefcase.

"The art department doesn't feel that this plan addresses the NAEA accreditation requirements," said Jeffries.

"But it does," I insisted. "You said so."

"I realized later that it didn't," he replied curtly.

I didn't have the NAEA documents to prove that my way would work. I had trusted Jeffries to bring them to the meeting. What a fool I was.

"Call the question," said Jeffries.

"But...." I protested.

"The question has been called," said the subcommittee chairman. "All in favor of the art department's proposal signify by saying 'Aye.'"

All but one member of the subcommittee voted for Jeffries's proposal; that person abstained. I was almost in tears.

"Dr. Lombardi," said the chairman, looking pityingly at me. "You will have another chance to propose your alternative program at the university committee. Make sure you bring fifty copies of it with you at that time."

I sat in silent fury through the rest of the meeting.

"I can't believe you did that to me, Scott," I said as we were leaving the conference room.

"Don't take it personally, my dear," he replied. "It's just university politics." And he waved a cheery good-bye as he headed out of the building.

I slunk back to my office and found Nanette waiting for me.

"How did it go?" she asked.

"Like a lamb to the slaughter, that's me. Oh, Nanette, he acted like we had never had those meetings. He just presented the original proposal."

"I was afraid of something like that. It all seemed too easy. Well, I'll tell the dean, and you get your counterproposal ready for the big committee meeting.

"I'm so sorry, Nanette."

She patted me on the shoulder. "Don't beat yourself up, Susan. You couldn't know what a piece of work Jeffries was. Even I didn't think he would pull something like this. We've lost the battle but not the war."

Despite her reassurances, I felt utterly defeated. I stared out my window, wishing that I hadn't been so gullible, wondering when I would become accustomed to the cutthroat politics of university life. Wintonbury had been such a small close-knit community; it was easy to know who was your friend and who wasn't. At Metropolitan, I was constantly meeting new people, all of them with their own agendas, some more hidden than others.

I looked up at the clock. It was four P.M. and there was Mark at the door to my office.

"Eureka!" he called. "I've found him!"

"Mark! You did? Wow, I could certainly use some good news about now. Tell me!"

"His name is Harvey Konigsberg. He spells it without the *e* in the 'konigs' part, and he's got an office in Queens. And I'm going to meet him there tomorrow for an interview."

"That's fabulous. How did you do it?"

"Just like I said. The Yellow Pages under 'accountants.' First I tried Brooklyn and there were a few with a number of different spellings of Konigsberg, but none of them had ever heard of Sabena. Then I tried Queens, and sure enough there was old Harvey. He said he'd read about her death in the *New York Times* but didn't think it concerned him, so he didn't get in touch with the police or anything. He also said he'd be happy to talk about her, but only in person. Seemed like a nice guy, soft-spoken, reasonable.

"Mark, this is sensational! What time is our appointment?"

"*Our* appointment? Don't you have classes tomorrow?"

"Only one. I'll get someone to cover it. I wouldn't miss this for anything. And besides, I could use a day in New York and some time away from here."

A nice, reasonable Harvey Konigsberg seemed like a big improvement over a smug, deceitful Scott Jeffries.

CHAPTER TWENTY

"Talk low, talk slow, and don't say too much."
John Wayne, *Advice on acting*

We found the office building on Queens Boulevard easily enough. Finding a parking space was more difficult, but we arrived at the office of Harvey Konigsberg, CPA, right on time. The building was small but well-maintained and housed a number of other professional offices. It looked as if Sabena's ex was doing all right without her.

The plump and pleasant receptionist told us that we were expected and showed us right into his office.

"Oh, there are two of you," he said, exhibiting very little surprise. "I expected only Mr. Goldin."

"I'm Susan Lombardi," I said, quickly offering a handshake. "I work with Mark."

He rose from his desk to shake my hand. Twenty years ago, he might have looked like Woody Allen. His hair, what was left of it anyway, was red, and his old-fashioned horn-rimmed glasses sat atop a prominent nose. But he was quite a large man. I imagined taking a bicycle pump and inflating Woody Allen like a balloon. The result would be Harvey Konigsberg.

Mark indicated the small tape recorder that he had brought with him. "Do you mind if we use this?" he asked.

"No problem. I have nothing to hide."

"Would you tell us about your relationship to Sabena?" I asked eagerly.

Harvey blinked. "There was no such person as Sabena Lazlo," he said quietly.

"What? What do you mean? You were married to her. You told Mark!"

Mark interrupted, "Susan, I think we should let him tell this his own way."

"Of course," I agreed. "I'm sorry, Mr. Konigsberg."

"Call me Harvey. Everyone does." We nodded our agreement, then waited for him to continue. It was probably thirty seconds before he began again, but it seemed like forever.

"There was no Sabena Lazlo. She was born as plain old Sheila Lattanzio." My eyes were probably popping out of my head, but I bit my tongue to keep from interrupting him. I wanted to show Mark that I could do this PI thing too.

"She was born in Brooklyn, just like me. She was an only child. Her mom was Jewish, her father Italian. They had a little neighborhood candy store. Such nice folks, and they treated Sheila like she was a princess. They're both gone now, of course." He paused. "Can I get either of you some coffee?"

We refused, hoping that this would hasten the process. We were wrong. Harvey got up and helped himself to coffee, cream, and sugar from a table behind his desk.

"I met Sheila in junior high school. I was a K and she was an L. She sat right behind me in all our classes. I think I fell in love with her the first day of seventh grade."

He took a long sip of his coffee and resumed. "Sheila was pretty and smart. And had so much energy. I never had half her energy." Another long pause while Harvey considered that fact. "We went through Midwood High School together, in all the same classes. I finally asked her out for the junior prom. I was surprised that no one else had asked her first, but I think a lot of the guys were afraid of her. She was so smart."

He looked out the window, obviously remembering his junior prom and how pretty and smart his Sheila had been. Even

Mark could take it no longer. "You went out with her for a long time, I suppose?" he asked.

"Yes," Harvey mused. "A long time. All the rest of junior year and all through senior year at Midwood. We both got into Brooklyn College, and I thought we'd go there together too."

"But you didn't?" I asked.

"Well, I went there. Sheila got a scholarship to Barnard. She was so thrilled about it. I pleaded with her to stay in Brooklyn with me, but she saw the scholarship as her ticket out of Brooklyn."

"So, she did go to Barnard!"

"Yes, she did. But we kept dating. At least freshman year. Then she dropped me for a while. I think she started going out with some Ivy League, Columbia guy."

"This was when?"

"Well, we graduated from Midwood in 1967. So somewhere in there, 1969 or 1970. Anyway, he must have broken her heart, because she came back to me. We got engaged at the end of our senior year in college and married a year later when Sheila finished her coursework at Penn."

"So she graduated from Barnard College in 1971, just as she said! But as Sheila Lattanzio." I said this more to myself than to anyone else.

"Yeah, and she never took my name. Right after Barnard, she went to court and had her name changed to Sabena Lazlo. I didn't understand it at the time, but I didn't care. I was so happy to be getting married to her." Again, his gaze drifted off.

"Where did the name Sabena Lazlo come from?" asked Mark.

"Huh? Oh, that. Well, while she was at Barnard, she spent a lot of time at the Thalia, you know the movie theater near Columbia that showed old films? She became a big Bogart fan. Dragged me to all his movies. She thought they were very romantic. I liked them too, I guess, but she was crazy about them. 'Lazlo' is one of the characters in *Casablanca*."

"Of course, the Paul Henreid character," I agreed. "But what about the *Sabena* part?"

"Yes, well, that was supposed to be 'Sabrina' — like the movie with Bogart and Audrey Hepburn? But then Sheila thought that might be too obvious, so she went for 'Sabena'— like the Belgian airline? She thought that would be exotic too. I remember her sitting at my mom's kitchen table making up all these names and trying them out on me. See how she kept the first and last letter of both her names? Sheila to Sabena, Lattanzio to Lazlo? She was so smart."

"And how long were you married?" I couldn't stand to hear even one more time about how smart and pretty she had been.

Harvey sighed and drained his coffee cup. "Let's see. She got a teaching job at that fancy Marston School in the fall soon after we were married and started moving in a snobbier crowd. She'd gotten rid of her Brooklyn accent while she was at Barnard. It was just a matter of time before she got rid of Brooklyn entirely, me included. We lasted about three years, although she wasn't around much the last year."

"And when did you hear from her last?" Mark asked.

Harvey took off his glasses and rubbed his eyes. He looked weary from his efforts to remember. "I think it was right before she left New York to go to Virginia. She called to tell me she'd gotten her Ph.D. and was going to marry this real WASPy guy."

"And you never heard from her again?"

"No. I read about her in the paper once, when she got to be head of that ritzy girls' school in New England. And now she's dead. Poor Sheila."

"You weren't angry all these years for what she did to you?"

Harvey smiled wistfully. "No," he said. "Sheila did what she had to do. She was too big a person for me, if you know what I mean." Unfortunately, I did know.

"And I did okay for me too. I like my work. I've got a nice home here in Forest Hills, just five minutes from my office. Two kids. And a very happy marriage. That's my wife you met at the receptionist's desk."

We thanked Harvey for his time, and as we went out, we wished a very warm goodbye to the second Mrs. Harvey Konigsberg.

CHAPTER TWENTY-ONE

"The best liar is he who makes the smallest
amount of lying go the longest way."
Samuel Butler, *The Way of All Flesh*

"So what do you think of ol' Harvey?" asked Mark, once we were back in the car. He was suppressing a grin.

"Well, I think we can eliminate him from our list of suspects," I answered, not even trying to hold back my smile. "He wouldn't have had the energy to travel to Wintonbury. And, seriously, I don't think he holds a grudge against Sabena for leaving him. So he wouldn't have a motive to kill her."

"I don't know." Mark tilted his head sideways as he thought. "Maybe he's a multiple personality — kind of like the Boston Strangler."

"Okay, let's keep Harvey's alter ego on our suspect list. But, Mark, are we obligated to tell the Wintonbury police about Harvey?"

"Tell them what about Harvey?"

"About his existence, I mean."

He furrowed his eyebrows as he looked out the window. "Hmm, not legally obligated, I think. But morally obligated, maybe."

"And so, will you?"

His face brightened suddenly. "Perhaps I can trade this little tidbit to Caz. In exchange for some info on how the police case is going."

"Caz?"

"Caz Czaikowski, my old friend from my University of New Haven days. He's the guy I mentioned who's with the Winton-bury PD."

"Maybe you can trade Richard Westcott to them for something too. We really don't have time to try to track him down somewhere in Virginia, do we? Assuming he still is in Virginia, of course."

"Susan, you're not giving up, are you?" Mark looked disappointed. He must have been more heavily invested in this case than I had realized.

"No, I don't mean that. It's just that our resources are so limited compared to the police. Maybe we should just stick to Wintonbury faculty after all."

"Gee, I think ol' Harvey really got to you."

"No, it's not that," I said. "Although I did find his whole story pretty depressing."

"But he's happy now. It all turned out just fine for him."

"No, it's not depressing for *him*. But think about Sabena — she made her whole life up. What was so wrong about being Sheila Lattanzio, do you think?"

"It wasn't her whole life she made up. She really did go to Barnard. She really did teach at Marston. It's only Brooklyn she got rid of."

"I suppose you're right, but it depresses me, nonetheless. How about we focus back on Wintonbury for a while? Feel like doing some work at Wintonbury?"

His gray eyes lit up. "Maybe. What do you have in mind?"

"I think we should focus on Rob Fleming. I want to find out about this student who's sneaking in and out of his back door at night."

"Prurient interest? Or something to do with the case?"

I elbowed him in the ribs — probably not a great idea since he was driving pretty fast. "The case, of course. Perhaps we can question her once we find out who she is. She might have seen something in her late night jaunts. How about doing a surveillance on Rob?"

"Let me give that a little thought," he replied. "It's been some time since I actually did a surveillance, and I never much enjoyed doing it."

I was surprised by his sudden hesitancy but didn't question it. After the excitement of locating Harvey Konigsberg, the reality of Sabena's life and the finality of her death seemed to cast a pall on our investigation.

We rode for nearly fifteen minutes in silence.

"Funny how Harvey still thinks of her so lovingly, isn't it?" Mark asked at last.

"Mm-hmm," I agreed. "People sure are unpredictable when it comes to long-lost loves." I thought about this for awhile. "Mark, why have you never married — if you don't mind my asking? Is there a long-lost love in your life?"

He stared fixedly at the road. "Well, there have been girlfriends along the way, but long-lost loves? No. I guess I just never met the right woman."

"That's so sad, Mark. But don't give up. Maybe she'll come along."

We spent the rest of our journey home listening to the radio and not talking much.

Later that evening, Swash asked, "Why so blue?"

"It just seems so sad that she couldn't just be Sheila Lattanzio and get on with her life," I said.

"All she did was change her name," he protested.

"No, she did more. She got rid of Brooklyn. She got rid of Harvey."

"It didn't sound like they were very well-matched to begin with."

I ignored that remark. He was being reasonable again. "She put on that slightly European accent...."

"She probably copied that from Paul Henreid too," he chuckled.

"What was so wrong with being Sheila Lattanzio? Her parents adored her. Harvey adored her. Maybe it was that Ivy League guy who broke her heart. What do you think, Swash?"

"I think you actually feel sorry for Sabena."

"I guess I do. Oh, my God."

"What is it?"

"Swash, I could have *been* Sabena. I grew up near New York. My father was Italian and my mother was Jewish."

"Susan, you grew up in suburban New Jersey — a far cry from Brooklyn." He gave me a stern look. "And your parents didn't own a candy store. They were schoolteachers."

"Yes, but...."

"And you liked who you were. No need to change your name or hide your past."

"And I'm not tall and chic with sleek black hair, either. But you're missing my point."

He came over and kissed the top of my head. "No, you're little and cute and your hair is a curly black mop. What *is* your point?"

"I might have liked Sheila Lattanzio, if I'd met her. We probably had a lot in common once."

"But you hated Sabena Lazlo. You hated her pretentiousness and her snobbery."

"And her ideas about what Wintonbury Academy should be. I know, I know. It's just...."

"That you're feeling sorry for her now because that Columbia guy jilted her twenty years ago?"

"Can it be that simple? I don't know, Swash. I just never thought of myself as having anything in common with her before."

"What difference does that make?"

I couldn't explain it to him. I couldn't explain it to myself either, but I was disappointed that Swash didn't understand anyway.

"I don't know," I admitted sheepishly. "I'm just identifying with her a bit too much, I guess."

"How about forgetting this investigation for a while? It's not too late for me to slip into something more comfortable, you know."

"But...."

"You're *not* Sabena. You never were. You lived your whole life as Susan Lombardi and did just fine. No glamorous, phony names. No affected accents." He stopped for a moment and smiled. "And you married me, of course."

I had to smile back at that. "Of course," I said. "That's the best part, isn't it?"

But I didn't sleep well that night. By breakfast time, I was more determined than ever to find the person who had murdered poor Sabena.

CHAPTER TWENTY-TWO

"My duty is to obey orders."
Stonewall Jackson, *A favorite aphorism*

Poor Sabena? Did I say that?

"Poor Sheila," maybe — the Sheila who hated herself so much that she made up another identity. But "poor Sabena?" Never.

Before I could get back to my "research" at Wintonbury, I had my life at Metropolitan to attend to. I came into my office at the university and found a note on my door from the dean. He wanted to see me immediately. Uh-oh.

"So I guess you heard about the fiasco with Scott Jeffries?" I asked as I entered the dean's office.

"Mm-hmm," he replied, barely looking up from his computer.

"Isn't that why you wanted to see me?"

"Sure, Susan. Have a seat, and wait just a moment while I save this stuff." He hit a few keys, then turned to face me. Harold Simonds was a man in his early sixties, bald with a fringe of white hair over each ear. He had a disarming smile that helped put faculty and students alike at their ease.

"I just wanted you to know that what happened in that subcommittee meeting wasn't about you," he began.

"Whew, it sure felt like me who was being humiliated," I said.

"Well, yes, it was, and I'm sorry for that. But it was me that Jeffries was after."

"I'm not sure I follow that."

"I'm new this year, right? And those old boys who chair the various departments...."

"And have chaired them since time immemorial...."

"Exactly. They think they have the power around here. But they don't. I'm the dean, and no teaching program gets approved at this university without my signature."

"Yes, but...."

"So they're just testing me, see? They have to see if I'm just a wimp they can push around."

"Oh." I thought for a moment. "So do you want to go to the big committee meeting in my place?"

"Nope," he replied. "I want you to go, armed to the teeth with your alternative program, the NAEA requirements, anything else that's relevant. Be prepared for a fight."

"Hal, I'm not sure I'm the one to do this."

"It'll be good practice for you, Susan," he laughed. "And if you lose the vote again, don't worry."

"Don't worry?"

"Yeah, don't worry. The president will never sign off on Jeffries's program if I don't approve it. So even if he wins, he loses."

"Then this whole thing is a charade?"

He shrugged. "I suppose you could call it that."

"But why?"

"Beats me. It's something about giving faculty a voice, I guess. That's university politics." With that he turned back to his computer.

I spent the morning going over my alternative program and the NAEA sheets that Jeffries's secretary had given me. I was sure that my program covered all the requirements.

But what did it matter? This was just an empty exercise so a bunch of gray-haired men could display their territorial imperatives, as far as I could tell. And yet I might make a real enemy in Jeffries. What if he retaliated when I came up for tenure? Could the dean protect me then?

I looked at the clock. The morning had flown by, and I was scheduled to meet with Granny Smith at noon.

Since this was a week when most of my Metropolitan students were "out in the field," visiting the classes and teachers with whom they would soon be student teaching, I had plenty of time to do my own visiting at Wintonbury. Granny had set me up with a class schedule that included most of the teachers and students whom I wanted to observe.

When I arrived at Wintonbury, Chuck Harris waved me through as I parked in the visitors' lot. Granny was sitting in her office with Melinda Collingswood, chairperson of the Board of Trustees. Melinda was dressed in the standard trustee uniform — a tailored Armani suit with Hermes scarf — and wore no makeup. Her blonde-gray pageboy was held back by a black velvet ribbon.

"Hello, Susan," she said. "Granny tells me that you are doing a little extra research for us these days."

"I don't know who it's for, Melinda. I just know that John wouldn't have hurt Sabena."

"That's what I've been assuring Melinda too," put in Granny. "In fact, I don't think it's anyone on our faculty."

"The board certainly doesn't want to think that we've been harboring a killer here," said Melinda with a shudder. "But we don't like the idea of a random killer either. What does that say about the safety of our students?"

"Well, we have stepped up security a lot," Granny said.

"That's not enough. We want to show that this crime was a one-of-a-kind, and aimed only at Sabena. But not by anyone associated with Wintonbury, of course."

"That's a tall order," said Granny.

"Yes, I guess so," Melinda admitted. "What do you think, Susan?"

"I agree with Granny that it might be hard to find the person to fit your specifications. You're saying that the ideal killer would be someone outside Wintonbury who knew Sabena before she came here?"

"Exactly. Now what have you found out so far?"

"Not a lot. I have met Sabena's first husband."

"And?"

"I'd cross him off the suspects list, I'm afraid." I described Harvey Konigsberg to them.

Melinda looked deflated. Then she brightened. "First husband? So there was a second?"

"Yes, I have his name, but I haven't found a way to locate him yet."

Granny raised an eyebrow. "It seems to me that that should be work for a private investigator, Susan. Couldn't the board hire an investigator of its own, Melinda? Surely the money is there?"

"Of course, the money is there, that's not the point. I'm worried about involving a complete stranger in Wintonbury matters. It's bad enough that we have the police asking all these questions."

"Well then, why not hire someone on a very limited basis?" suggested Granny. "Someone who would do background checks and the like, but who would stay away from Wintonbury — not come on campus and not ask questions of anyone here."

"I suppose that might be a compromise," said Melinda. "My husband's law firm does have someone whom they use to do things like that. What is the name of the second husband, Susan? We'll see if this investigator can find him."

"Richard Westcott," I replied. "He was a professor of education in Virginia somewhere. But when I checked the Internet telephone directory, there were forty-four Richard Westcotts in the US and not one in Virginia."

Melinda made a note of that and then, with a gracious goodbye, hurried from Granny's office.

I looked at Granny who was smiling broadly. "Well, that should speed things up a bit, Susan. You really don't have the resources for this, you know."

"Yes, but...."

"And just because Melinda and the board want the murderer to be someone off-campus doesn't mean it is, does it?"

"No, but...."

"So suppose you just keep at your research here on campus? Okay, Susan?"

"Yes, and...."

"And you just make sure that you report back to me if you find anything really interesting." Granny winked at me. "Now hurry off to chemistry class, dear."

CHAPTER TWENTY-THREE

"You can observe a lot by watching."
Yogi Berra, *Remark*

I trudged off to Harper Hall, where I was to observe the chemistry class. The pungent smells of the science laboratories brought a wave of nostalgia as I entered Harper again. I had spent ten years teaching amid the odors and clutter of those labs.

Barbara Gordon, the chemistry teacher, was busy helping a particularly inept duo with a titration as I entered, but she looked up and managed a smile. She was one of those people who seemed plain until she smiled. Then her face lit up with a sweetness that was hard to resist.

The students, all in pairs, were concentrating on their burets and barely noticed me. Their long hair tied back with rubber bands, plastic goggles covering intent eyes, and plastic aprons over sweatshirts and jeans, they looked just like the Wintonbury girls whom I fondly remembered.

Scanning the room, I spotted the two girls I had come to observe: Punkin Brady and Liza Ledyard. Granny had told me that they were both in this class, and that they were inseparable friends. Experience told me that they would probably be lab partners if given the chance. And experience was right.

With auburn hair, pale skin dotted with freckles, and the athletic build that made her Wintonbury's star soccer player, Punkin was easy to identify. She was carefully turning the stopcock, her brow furrowed in concentration, while her more laid-back partner took notes in her lab notebook. Liza was smaller than Punkin, slightly built, and much more glamorous, with high cheekbones, long chestnut hair, and a remarkable tan, no doubt from a Christmas vacation in Antigua or Aruba.

Barbara introduced me to the class, then turned her attention to the students. I roamed the laboratory, stopping a few minutes at each pair to listen to their conversations and take notes. The girls smiled politely at me and went back to their work. I managed to arrive at Punkin and Liza near the end of the period and lingered behind them as they cleaned up their experiment.

"Hi," said Punkin, acknowledging my presence when class ended. Without goggles, her near-white eyebrows and lashes made a striking frame for straightforward brown eyes that looked boldly into mine. "Shauna told us you were investigating the Empress's murder. Shauna thinks you suspect one of the students."

I gasped slightly. "I didn't say that."

Liza smiled sweetly as the three of us ambled out of the lab. "Shauna's very smart. She figures things out. So which one of us do you suspect?"

It took me just a moment to recover from this. Years of teaching adolescents had given me the knack of quickly bouncing back from the most outrageous statements.

"Well, Shauna figured that one out wrong," I replied with a grin. "I think one of you may have seen something important and doesn't realize it, but I don't think any of you murdered Dr. Lazlo."

"How could we have seen anything? We're all locked up after ten o'clock," Punkin said.

"Don't some of you leave the dorm after you've checked in at ten?" I asked, delighted by the opportunity to put the question so directly.

I saw that same exchange of looks that I had seen pass between Tiffany and Shauna a few days earlier.

"We're not supposed to," said Liza.

"But I guess *some* girls might," Punkin added.

"And do you know who some of those girls might be?" I tried to keep my face calm and expressionless.

"No, none of our friends would do that! And Liza and I are already on probation, so we certainly wouldn't risk it."

"Probation for what?"

"Oh, that silly drinking incident with Tiffany and Shauna," Liza answered. "I guess you heard about that."

"We're lucky that we weren't suspended!" said Punkin. "Mr. Lyons went easy on us."

"What was Dr. Lazlo going to do? Would she have suspended you?"

Another exchange of looks. "Maybe," Liza replied at last. "She just said she'd have to think about it."

"Then she was murdered." Punkin shivered a little as she spoke.

"Had she suspended other girls for similar offenses?"

"I think so, but you never could tell what the Empress would do. If she were having a really bad day, she might even decide to expel a girl for drinking. Listen, Dr. Lombardi, Liza and I have to get to another class."

"We're late already," Liza added.

I waved good-bye to them and watched them run down the hill to the Theatre and Art Building. If I were lucky, they'd be in one of Elaine's classes, and she would know much more about them. Students confided in Elaine.

The guilty look on Punkin's open face told me that students were sneaking out of the dormitories at night. One of them, I guessed, was going to Rob Fleming's house, but were there others? And where were they going? There were longstanding rumors about secret ceremonies in the night, but none of the faculty ever knew for sure. I'd have to convince Mark to do that surveillance soon.

The rest of the day was spent watching classes. I saw Rob Fleming flirt indiscriminately with half of his seniors as they discussed Keats. "Thou still unravish'd bride of quietness" aroused some giggles, while "For ever panting and for ever young" evoked raucous laughter. Rob led them next to consider whether "Beauty is truth, truth beauty."

"Watson and Crick thought their DNA model was so beautiful that it had to be true. Miss Gordon was just telling us about that," said one of the girls.

"But sometimes the truth is ugly, not beautiful," said Nini, a challenge in her eyes.

"And sometimes we tell lies to keep things from getting ugly," put in Mandy.

A spirited discussion of truth and deceit ensued, until Rob steered them back to a consideration of beauty and what Keats meant in the final lines of the poem. I could see why, good looks aside, the girls idolized him

I watched Alan Lyons teach an uninspired history class. The topic was the Civil War, and he droned on about military strategies, all the while ignoring the stifled yawns and glazed expressions of the girls in the class. Alan had dark circles under his eyes and clearly was too busy doing extra administrative tasks to prepare much for the one class he taught.

The inevitable question came midway through the class: "Is this going to be on the test?"

"You better believe it," replied Alan, with a scowl.

I watched Elaine energetically directing a group of girls who were rehearsing *Death*, a one act play by Woody Allen. The student playing the Maniac was overacting.

"Understate the lines, Jennifer," said Elaine.

"But I'm a maniac," the girl protested.

"You don't get it," said the student playing Kleinman. "You look like me. You are just ordinary. That makes you even scarier as a killer, get it?"

"Good point," said Elaine. "I do think that makes it scarier, but also funnier, don't you think? That a killer can be so ordinary — look just like one of us?"

"Is that what Woody Allen meant?" asked the girl called Jennifer.

Woody Allen. I thought about Harvey Konigsberg again. And my conversation with Mark on the return trip from New York.

I called Mark as soon as I got home.

"Mark, you've got to do that surveillance right away!"

"Susan, I've got that Radinsky paper."

"How about tomorrow night? You can finish the paper tonight and...."

"Uh, I think I better tell you something."

"Yes?"

"I told you I hadn't done much surveillance, right? What I didn't tell you was that the last time I did do one, I was arrested."

A minor omission.

CHAPTER TWENTY-FOUR

"As I in hoary winter night stood shivering in the snow
Surprised was I with sudden heat which
made my heart to glow."
Robert Southwell, *The Burning Babe*

"Arrested! Mark, how did that happen?"

"It was when I was working for the insurance companies. I was watching a disability claimant. I'd parked my car by the woods on the Avon-Simsbury line to watch the house, and the next thing I knew there was this badge in my face. I finally got it straightened out at the Simsbury police station, but it wasn't much fun."

"Hmm, is there some way we can avoid a repeat of that little misadventure?"

"Yeah, I'll talk to Caz and have him clear this for me. Speaking of Caz...."

"Yes? Did you give him the information about Harvey and Westcott?"

"Indeed, I did. They're going to check on Harvey's alibi and try to find Westcott. I've got to tell you Caz wasn't too impressed, though. They're pretty sure the killer is at the school."

I groaned. "That must mean they still suspect John."

"I'm afraid so. Now about this surveillance ...."

"How's Monday night? Will the Radinsky paper be done?"

"I expect so. Now, whose house am I watching, and where is it?"

"Rob Fleming's house on Brook Street. I'll show you where it is when we...."

"We? Who said anything about we? This is *my* job." He sounded pretty firm.

"But I'm the one who will recognize the girl. And besides, you can't have all the fun!"

"Fun? Sitting in a cold car? Going hours without a bathroom?"

That stopped me for a moment. "How about for just a few hours? Say, eleven to two in the morning? I suspect those are the relevant hours, and I can last that long."

Mark sighed. "Okay. I'll try to clear it with Caz."

And so it was that Mark and I found ourselves sitting in his little Metro on Academy Street late one February night. From this position we could keep our eyes on Brook Street, where Rob and the Trouts lived. We could also detect any movement down from Dormitory Hill. It was a clear, cold night, and we were both bundled up in turtlenecks and down jackets.

Naturally, Swash had been less than overjoyed about my accompanying Mark on this late night excursion. For my part, I was feeling a little disappointed at Swash's failure to support my latest whim. This is undoubtedly why, as Mark and I huddled together in the cold, I felt a new sensation pass between us. Mark understood me. Mark understood the adventure of our quest. Mark....

Mark was caressing my hair, my neck.

Uh-oh.

I pulled away.

"This is not good," I said. "It's definitely not good for the relationship."

"Which relationship?" he asked softly.

"Yours and mine. Our professional relationship. Teacher, student. Co-investigators. Mine and Swash's. All of the above." I was babbling.

"Mmmmm," he said, nuzzling closer.

Suddenly, I saw a figure moving down Dormitory Hill.

"Mark, give me the binoculars!"

Mark backed away quickly and reached for the binoculars. I grabbed them and got a closer look.

The girl headed behind the faculty houses. As she passed beneath a campus light, I could just make out her face and long dark hair. It was Mandy Lewis, Wintonbury senior and friend of Nini Westmore.

Mandy! That meant that Rob Fleming was "the slime."

Well, I always knew that.

CHAPTER TWENTY-FIVE

"Fasten your seatbelts. It's going to be a bumpy night."
Joseph L. Mankiewicz, *All About Eve*

I reached for the handle of the car door, ready to pursue Mandy across campus if need be. But Mark held my arm.

"Don't go after her!" he warned in a hoarse whisper. "You don't know yet where's she's going. Sit tight and watch."

He was right, of course. So we sat. We didn't talk. We stared out the windows, carefully avoiding looking at one another. We saw Mandy go behind Rob's house and enter the back door, obviously left unlocked. We sat some more.

At a few minutes after midnight, the front porch light went on at John deHavilland's house across the street. What was this? John should be asleep or in bed reading a history book.

It was Barbara Gordon, the chemistry teacher, and she was reaching up to kiss someone good-night. Hmm. John hadn't told me about this. Or was it the first time? Was there something erotic in the air this frigid February night? I tried not to think about that.

"Wow! What busy faculty they have here!" whispered Mark, smiling broadly.

"Shh!" I hissed.

Barbara strode briskly down Brook Street and turned into the path leading up the hill. I knew she had a small apartment in one of the dormitories. Barbara and John? Well, perhaps he was not as alone as I'd assumed.

Twenty minutes later, we saw the light turn on in Harry Trout's kitchen. Why was everyone up so late? They had early morning classes to teach.

"Must be insomniac Harry," I said. "He's going for his warm milk. Or a shot of whiskey."

"Or maybe he's just going to spy on Rob Fleming. See, the light's out again, but you can still see him standing there." Mark pointed into the darkness.

I could dimly make out Harry's stocky silhouette behind the kitchen door.

"The old busybody!"

Mark chuckled. "What does that make us, Susan?"

My answer was an elbow in his ribs.

"Ouch! The woman has no sense of humor! Good thing I'm wearing this down jacket."

"Shh. Look!"

A shadowy figure was moving behind the houses again. This time Mark didn't restrain me. I shoved the car door open and ran quickly across the backyards. I overtook her easily.

"Mandy!" I gasped, grabbing at her arm. She tried to pull away, but I held firmly to her. "It's Dr. Lombardi. I'm not going to report you. Just talk to me a minute."

She looked like a deer caught in the headlights. Eyes open wide, she stood shivering in the cold night air. I pulled her into an unlighted area so that Harry, if he were still watching, couldn't see our faces.

"Dr. Lombardi! Why are you here? Please don't tell anyone!" Tears began to form in her eyes.

"I already said I won't report you, Mandy. Although I do agree with Nini that you shouldn't be seeing that sleaze."

"Slime," Mandy corrected.

"Whatever. The point is he is a rotten little person."

"But so handsome and romantic. He...."

"Ugh. Don't tell me about it." I shuddered. "You need to get back to your dorm right away. Will you have trouble getting back in?"

"No, we have a system worked out. Nini will let me in."

"Okay, Mandy, I'll let you go, and I won't tell anyone about this."

"Oh, thank you, Dr. Lombardi!"

I held her arm tightly. "But you must promise to talk to me tomorrow afternoon when I'm back on campus."

"Oh, please!" she said. "No lectures on safe sex."

"Good lord, I hope that's not necessary. No, I want to talk about the night of Dr. Lazlo's murder."

"But I didn't see anything that night!"

"So you *were* out that night. That's what I thought." Mark had told me that people often reveal more than you ask, but I was impressed with my sleuthing skills nonetheless. "Promise that you'll meet me at Nifty's tomorrow at four."

"Okay, Dr. Lombardi. I promise."

I gave her one last searching look. She seemed earnest, so I let her go. As she hurried away toward the dormitories, I returned to the car, keeping to the shadows as much as possible to avoid Harry's snooping eyes.

"Mission accomplished," I said to Mark as I got back in the car. "Let's go."

As Mark drove me home, we talked about Mandy and what I should ask her the next day. We studiously avoided discussing what had transpired between us.

Swash was already asleep when I came in. It was just as well. I had a lot of thinking to do.

CHAPTER TWENTY-SIX

"Three little maids from school are we,
Pert as a schoolgirl well can be,
Filled to the brim with girlish glee."
W.S. Gilbert. *The Mikado*

I was up early and left for school before Swash awoke, thereby avoiding, once again, the inevitable questions. The day dragged on and on. I ended my class early — at three forty-five — putting off two students who had questions about assignments. As I hurried to my car, I had a fleeting flash of guilt at neglecting my Metropolitan students but resolutely pushed it away, telling myself that solving Sabena's murder was important work too.

When I arrived at Nifty's, the ice cream and sandwich shop frequented by Wintonbury students, it was filled with the chatter and giggles of dozens of adolescent girls. Mandy was waiting for me in a booth near the back. She had brought reinforcements: her best friend, Nini Westmore, and the formidable Shauna Thompson.

"I hope you don't mind that Nini and Shauna are here," she said, smiling sheepishly.

"Not so long as you all tell me the truth," I replied, returning her smile.

"I think we need to know where this information is going to go," said Shauna, not smiling at all.

"Sure, I can understand that. It won't go to the school, that I can promise. It might have to go to the police though, if it becomes important in solving Dr. Lazlo's murder."

"Hmm." Shauna looked thoughtful.

Nini brushed her flaxen hair out of her eyes. "Well, I didn't much like the Emp, but she didn't deserve to be murdered." She gave a determined nod and thrust out her chin. "I think we should help, guys."

"As long as we don't get in trouble," Shauna insisted.

"Well, okay," said Mandy, looking down at the dish of chocolate chip ice cream in front of her. "Here goes."

I waited patiently. I would have liked some ice cream too, but didn't want to call over the waitress and break the mood.

"See, I've been going to Rob's — Mr. Fleming's — house after hours for a few months now. I'm in my room at ten when Mrs. Lyons does check-in, but when she's done, I go out the back door and over to his house."

"There's no alarm on the doors on the inside," Nini added helpfully.

"Yeah, they trust us," said Shauna, finally breaking out her high power grin.

"Anyway, I usually get out about eleven or so and stay with Rob till one or one-thirty."

"Then I let her back in." Nini was clearly proud of this act of friendship, even if she didn't approve of the slime involved.

"And the night of the murder?" I prodded.

"I really didn't see anything different that night, I swear."

"Was anything different at all?"

Mandy looked uncertainly at Nini. Nini looked at Shauna, who nodded.

"Uh, well, I sort of fell asleep that night, and Rob said I was so beautiful lying there that he didn't want to wake me. He said I was kind of like the goddess of the dawn or something."

Nini, sitting beside her, made gagging noises.

"And so I didn't get back until much later than usual."

"It was after four in the morning, actually," said Shauna. "And meanwhile we were all hysterical about where you were."

"I was freaking," Nini explained. "When it got to be two in the morning, I didn't know what to do. I needed to get to sleep. I had this PreCal test the next day, but I didn't want to leave Mandy out there."

"So Nini was crying, and a bunch of us came to see what was wrong."

"And I guess we were making lots of noise, because Mr. Lyons came up from downstairs."

"And we couldn't tell *him* what the problem was."

"So he goes ballistic and tells us to get to bed."

"So we took shifts and sat up all night until Mandy finally came in!" Shauna concluded the duet.

"I felt really bummed about what happened," Mandy admitted. "But Nini did okay on her PreCal test, so I kind of forgot about the whole thing."

"And meanwhile, someone was murdering Dr. Lazlo," I said. "Somewhere between two and four in the morning, according to the police."

The three girls all shuddered, almost in unison.

"And none of you heard or saw anything unusual, you're sure?" I tried one last time, unwilling to give up with no new information to show for my trouble.

"Dr. Lazlo's office is pretty far from the dorms and faculty houses, you know," Nini explained. "We wouldn't have heard anything inside the dorm."

"I know I didn't see anyone else outside when I was going to Rob's or coming back," said Mandy firmly.

"Okay, thanks. Here, let me pay for your ice cream. And please, if you remember anything else, give me a call." I left them my business card.

On the way out I got myself a mocha chip cone with chocolate sprinkles.

CHAPTER TWENTY-SEVEN

"True friendship is never serene."
Marie de Rabutin-Chantal, Marquise de Sevigne, *Lettres*

"Did you see today's *Tribune?*" asked Elaine over wine that night. Around us, Buonarotti's was bustling as usual.

I nodded, sipping the beaujolais. *Townspeople Angered by Police Lack of Action*, the headline had said. The citizens of Wintonbury were understandably upset that two weeks had gone by and there had been no arrest of Sabena's killer.

"Too bad they didn't arrest Harvey Konigsberg. I was hoping to see his photo in the paper someday. Does he really look like Woody Allen?"

"There's a certain resemblance, yes. But I don't think the police have really checked anyone outside of Wintonbury." I was a little miffed that my big discovery of the existence of two ex-husbands was treated as so unimportant by the Wintonbury PD. "They're convinced it's one of you!"

The waiter, fawning over Elaine, took our order. Elaine rolled her eyes heavenwards when he finally left us alone.

"So what did you find out from the girls?" she asked.

"Not much. Mandy Lewis is Rob's latest."

"Poor Mandy." Elaine shook her head. "Beautiful, but a little dim. A perfect target for him."

"Yes," I agreed. "And she stayed at his house longer than usual that night, evidently throwing the dorm into an uproar when she didn't return at the appointed time."

"So she was with Rob when the murder occurred?" mused Elaine, raising an eyebrow. "Giving him an alibi if he should need it?"

"I suppose so. But if she fell asleep between one and four in the morning, maybe Rob could have slipped out, murdered Sabena, and returned without Mandy's knowing it."

"Thereby establishing an alibi. Clever, but how could he have been certain she would fall asleep?"

As Elaine raised her glass to her lips, I glanced at the bottle on the table between us. "Maybe he gave her some wine that night. Or more wine than usual, in any case."

"But," Elaine protested, "would he really set himself up with an alibi like that? Revealing that alibi would expose his late night lechery to one and all."

"Maybe not. He could tell the police. They wouldn't necessarily tell the school, would they? They might just wink at the whole thing — boys will be boys, you know."

Our orders of penne with sun-dried tomatoes arrived, and for a few minutes, pasta took precedence over murder.

"Even if the school found out and fired him, that's better than being arrested as a murderer," I continued, dabbing at my lips with my napkin. "After all, he's a published poet. Some other school would hire him."

"More's the pity. You're right, of course," Elaine conceded.

"Now, what about Alan Lyons?" I asked, moving down my mental list. "According to Shauna and Nini, he was scolding them about the noise they were making at two in the morning. So we know where he was at two."

"But he could have killed Sabena *after* two, couldn't he?" she said, her lustrous brown eyes narrowing with suspicion.

"Damn it, Elaine! What you're saying is that nothing I learned from Mandy and company is of any use at all. It doesn't eliminate either Rob or Alan from suspicion!"

"I suppose I am saying that."

"Well, have you heard anything from your students that might be useful?"

She shook her head. "They confide in me about their love lives mostly. I know about Punkin's lacrosse player at Stratford Hall and Liza's pre-med at Yale."

"How did you happen to mention those two? I was just about to ask you about them."

"I knew you were. They told me you were snooping around their chemistry class."

"Chemistry! That's what I had to tell you."

The waiter took our order for tiramisu and coffee and poured the remaining wine into Elaine's glass. He didn't seem to notice that mine was empty too.

"I think the waiter's getting up the nerve to ask you out," I whispered.

"I certainly hope not," she said, a smile on her lips nonetheless. "Now what's this about chemistry?"

"Barbara Gordon! I saw her giving John a fond farewell on his front porch the night I was doing the surveillance with Mark."

"Mousy little Barbara! Well, good for her! And for John too."

"So you didn't know about it either," I chuckled. "Yes, good for John. He certainly needs someone."

"Don't we all," she sighed. "And don't you dare mention the waiter again. So is John still the chief suspect, do you know?"

"According to Mark, yes. He is the only one who is known to have threatened her. But they are following the lead about the *Bartlett's Quotations* too."

Elaine gulped the last of her wine, and looked at me wide-eyed.

"What about *Bartlett's*?"

"Sabena's *Bartlett's Quotations*. It went missing sometime around the night she was murdered. The police think it may be a clue to the murderer's identity."

"Oh, no."

"Elaine?" She was several shades paler than her ivory silk blouse.

"But *I* took the *Bartlett's*! I thought you knew!"

CHAPTER TWENTY-EIGHT

"A good joke is the one ultimate and sacred
thing which cannot be criticized.
Our relations with a good joke are direct and
even divine relations."
G.K. Chesterton, *Preface to Dickens, Pickwick Papers*

"Elaine, how could I possibly know? I can't believe this!"

"But last time we were here, remember? We were talking about the pranks we'd played on old Mrs. Worthington?"

"Yes, but...."

"And you said no one would dare play a prank on Sabena? And I said that some of us had? Well, I assumed you would take it from there!"

"But I didn't hear about the *Bartlett's* until after that! And why should I have assumed it was you? Like everyone else, I assumed the murderer took it!"

Elaine's face fell. "Yes, and that's what the police are assuming, isn't it? I'm in big trouble."

"Elaine, how could you do something so foolish?" I tried to keep the exasperation I felt out of my voice.

"I couldn't very well have known she would get murdered that night, now could I?" she said indignantly. "And if she hadn't gotten herself murdered, it would have been a very funny prank, and we would all be laughing for weeks about how she couldn't give a speech without it."

"Yes, I suppose so. But she *was* murdered, and now your little joke isn't so funny. You have to go to the police and confess."

"Susan, I could never do that." She leaned forward and added in her best stage whisper, "You have to help me put the book back."

"Where is it now?" I asked, trying to ignore the uneasy feeling that I was getting myself involved in something I would regret.

"In a bookbag in the trunk of my car."

"And how did you get it out of Sabena's office in the first place?"

"Easy," Elaine replied with a sly smile. "You know that annoying way that Sabena had of answering phone calls while you were in there talking to her?"

"Yes, I remember. She would spin around in her desk chair and turn her back to you while she spoke, making you feel like you weren't there."

"Exactly. When she did that, I was already so furious with her about canceling the Shakespeare festival, that I decided it would be only justice to exact some revenge. And there was the *Bartlett's* sitting on the corner of her desk. And there was my bookbag sitting right on the floor next to her desk."

"You just took it while her back was turned?"

"As I said, easy. When she got off the phone, she just dismissed me in best Empress fashion and said she had another appointment. I smiled demurely and left, chuckling to myself. That was it. I never gave it another thought until after the murder. You have to admit that it was a good joke!"

"Yes, indeed, it was a very funny joke, until Sabena's murder ruined the fun. But how are you going to put it back?"

We sat sipping our decaf in silence.

"What if I were to pretend to find it in the theatre and bring it to Jane? Does anyone else know that it's missing?"

I thought for a moment. "Jane told me, and she also told the police. I don't know who else knows. I told John and Mark and Swash."

"So I could act completely innocent."

"Something you do so well."

"And no one would suspect that I actually took it!"

"But the police would certainly want to question you about it, since you would be the one who found it. Could you lie convincingly to the police, do you think?"

Elaine drew herself up to her full majestic height in the chair. "I *am* an actress, you know!"

Could she lie convincingly to me too? I wondered a moment about that, then said, "I think it would be better if someone else found it. And in some other building than the theatre, which is, after all, your domain."

"Yes, you're right. People would naturally think of me if it were found in the theatre. But where?" Another silence while we sipped and pondered.

"I've got it, Elaine! It's right out of Edgar Allen Poe and *The Purloined Letter*. Where would you hide a book?"

"In a library, of course! Very smart, Susan."

I smiled proudly at her praise. After a moment's thought, she continued, "I can go in there tomorrow morning — there are never any girls in the library before breakfast — and just slip it from my bookbag onto one of the shelves. But I need someone to make sure that the librarian on duty doesn't see me."

"So, you're thinking...."

"That you might just go to Wintonbury tomorrow morning on your way to Metropolitan and stop by the library for a visit."

"And why exactly would I do that?"

"To help me, what else? Oh, you mean what pretext can you give to the librarian?"

"Yes. It wasn't exactly my habit to drop into the library for a chat, even when I worked at Wintonbury. Why would I do it now?"

Elaine's eyes searched the ceiling for inspiration. "Hmm. How about to get her opinion on Sabena's murder? Everyone knows you're snooping around about that."

I swallowed hard. "Okay, Elaine, I'll do it. Just because you're my best friend. But you owe me, bigtime."

A look of relief passed over her face. Sighing slightly, she drained the rest of the decaf from her cup. I did the same, my mind racing.

"That's perfect," she said. "We'll hide the book tomorrow, and one of the librarians will find it misshelved in a day or two and bring it to Jane."

"No, *you'll* hide the book tomorrow," I corrected. "I'm merely keeping the librarian occupied, remember? Just make sure that you wipe your fingerprints off the book and handle it with gloves."

Elaine shuddered. "That sounds so criminal! But I suppose you're right. I don't want it traced back to me, do I?"

I shuddered in response. What if I were aiding and abetting a murderer?

CHAPTER TWENTY-NINE

"Words are easy like the wind;
Faithful friends are hard to find."
Richard Barnfield, *Poems: In Divers Humours*

I awoke the next morning in a terrible mood. All of my interviewing and sleuthing had led nowhere, as Elaine had so clearly pointed out. My night of surveillance with Mark had only led to a strain in our relationship, one that neither of us had the courage to discuss.

And what of John, who had involved me in this murder in the first place? Why, he was having a torrid affair that he hadn't even mentioned to me! And now I was afraid that Elaine was a murderer.

Then there was Swash. He still disapproved of my involvement in the case. How he would feel about my involvement with Mark, I didn't want to contemplate. And of course, I couldn't tell him about what I was about to do with Elaine. We had an unusually quiet breakfast, each of us buried in the newspaper as we sipped our coffee.

I tried to push all of this out of my mind as I drove to Wintonbury. I pulled into the visitors' lot, yet again—I was beginning to think that the word *visitor* no longer applied—and trekked up to the library. As predicted, there were no students around yet, but Elaine was waiting by the back door.

"You just go around the front," she said. "I'll give you about five minutes to find the librarian and start a conversation, then I'll slip in the back here."

"All right, but be quick about it. I can't promise to keep her occupied for long."

Elaine giggled nervously. "This is rather exciting, isn't it?"

"Nerve-racking is more like it," I whispered. "Let's get it over with."

I hurried around the side of the library and entered the front door. Laraine Marshall, one of the two Wintonbury librarians, was at her desk cataloging books.

"Susan, hello," she said looking up at me over her half-glasses. "I was wondering when you'd get around to me."

This isn't going to be too difficult, I thought to myself.

"Laraine, so you've heard I'm interviewing people."

"Yes, I can't imagine why you'd want to be involved in this whole sordid business, but *de gustibus*, I suppose."

"Do *you* have any theories about the murder, Laraine?" I asked, ignoring the implied insult.

"Well, I was at the faculty meeting where John threatened her."

"Not you too? You surely can't think that John...."

"No, I don't. Not really. But how can I suspect anyone? I've worked here for over twenty years, Susan. Nothing like this has ever happened here. Or to anyone I know. How does one make sense of something like a murder?"

"I don't know, Laraine," I replied. "I guess asking questions is my way of coping."

"And my way is to catalog books," she said, looking down at the pile on her desk.

I thought I heard the back door opening. Was Elaine coming in or going out?

"Just one more question," I said, stalling for time. "Did you notice anything different that morning when you got here? You must get to campus before almost anyone else."

"No, I didn't notice anything. The campus was empty. Chuck Harris was in his little kiosk keeping warm. I parked in my usual space, and everything seemed normal."

"Thanks, Laraine. I guess that's all. Good seeing you, although I wish it were under happier circumstances."

She waved good-bye and went back to her books. I went around the back and saw Elaine heading to the theatre.

"Susan!" she called. "Operation *Purloined Letter* went off without a hitch."

She sounded elated more than relieved, I thought to myself. "Shh," I replied. "I'm glad there was no problem."

"Really, Susan, it was so easy. Next time I need to plan a crime, I'll certainly come to you for help."

I groaned. "No more crimes, Elaine. Your criminal career has ended as of today."

"Too bad. But you're right, of course. See you next week. Cheers!"

She gave me a Cheshire cat grin and waved good-bye.

CHAPTER THIRTY

"Here lies my past. Good-bye I have kissed it.
Thank you kids. I wouldn't have missed it."
Ogden Nash, *You Can't Get There from Here*

Arriving at the university and, as usual, having to park in an ice-encrusted lot ten minutes from my building did not improve my mood. Rick Benedetto, reeking of stale smoke, greeted me at the photocopy machine. A perfect start to the day, I thought.

"Why, Rick," I said tartly, "making your own photocopies?"

"Yeah," he grumbled. "Marie's busy, and I couldn't find any of our student helpers to do it. What are their hours anyway?" Rick was notorious for his laziness. He was the only one in the department who refused to let a computer into his office for fear that he would then be asked to do his own typing. "I don't suppose that you ...."

"Not a chance, Rick." I glowered at him. What might have developed into a real argument was interrupted by the arrival of Laurie Nash, another of our colleagues. Petite and sweet-faced, with sandy hair and freckles, Laurie was a person who always made me feel that there was hope for Metropolitan University.

"My students are so good this semester," she began, her face glowing. "They just did so well on that first lesson plan assignment!"

"Hrrrumphhh. Not my students. A bunch of idiots, that's all I've got," Rick muttered.

"Now, Rick," Laurie said patiently. "They can't all be like that."

Rick finished his photocopying and left, still muttering under his breath.

"There's no point in arguing with Rick," I said. "Why do you bother?"

Laurie looked at me earnestly, her brown eyes wide. "You can't just give up on people, can you, Susan? I keep hoping ...."

"Some people aren't worth the effort, Laurie," I said. Then feeling guilty, I added, "My students are pretty wonderful too. But if you had Rick for a teacher, how hard would *you* work?"

At that point, the photocopier jammed. Perfect.

Laurie and I fixed the jam, and I went back to my desk to work on my committee presentation. Even though the dean had assured me that it really didn't matter what I said, I didn't want to be humiliated again. As I was putting the finishing touches on my proposal, the phone rang.

"Susan, it's Granny. Melinda's investigator has located Richard Westcott."

"Wow, that was fast."

I heard her chuckle. "A simple job for someone with the right resources, just as I said."

I sighed. "And you were right. So where is he?"

"He's a professor at Rutgers University, at their campus in Newark. Not nearly as far as Virginia. It would have been easy for him to have driven up here from New Jersey."

"Now who's getting involved where she has no professional expertise?" I asked.

"Oh, dear, it is easy to slip into that, isn't it?" she replied, laughing at herself. "Well, now that you know where he is, can you contact him?"

"Granny, I'll do that as soon as I hang up."

"I guess I can take a hint, Susan. Good-bye, and let me know what you find out."

I quickly got information and retrieved the number for the School of Education at Rutgers-at-Newark. At the same time, I checked their website for a way to contact Dr. Westcott. Whether by high tech or low tech means, I was determined to reach him.

Low tech triumphed. The main switchboard at his university put me through to Westcott's office, and he was there.

"Dr. Westcott," I began. "My name is Susan Lombardi, and I'm a professor of education at Metropolitan University in Connecticut."

"Are you calling about the literacy conference?" he asked. "Because if you are, you...."

"No, not about the conference. I'm calling about Sabena Lazlo."

"Who is this?" His tone was sharp.

I repeated my name and position.

"Sabena and I were divorced years ago," he replied. "I did read about her death, of course, but that had nothing to do with me."

"Yes, of course," I assured him. "But I am doing some work for the school she was at — Wintonbury — just putting together a fuller picture of who she was for, uh, their memorial to her, and I would be so grateful if I could interview you." Whew! I was starting to get good at making things up as I went along.

"Well, I suppose that would be all right. We did part amicably, although we haven't kept up with one another."

"Oh that's wonderful! Do you have time tomorrow?" I looked at my calendar — no classes tomorrow and no research scheduled. I could just cancel my office hours and head to New Jersey.

We made a date for the following afternoon at a little coffee shop just off the New Jersey Turnpike.

* * *

Richard Westcott was there when I arrived. He wasn't tall — maybe an inch shorter than Sabena had been — but he was extremely attractive. Pure white hair and startling blue eyes set off a patrician face. Sabena had certainly married up from Harvey Konigsberg.

"Dr. Westcott, thank you so much for seeing me at such short notice."

"Dr. Lombardi, it's a pleasure to meet you," he replied, "although the circumstances are tragic, of course."

"Yes," I agreed. I ordered some coffee and an English muffin from an amiable waitress. The formalities over, I launched right in. "Tell me about Sabena when you knew her."

"Sabena was a grad student when I met her. She was teaching at Marston School. Do you know it?"

I nodded. "It's a pretty famous school," I said.

"Yes," he agreed. "Sabena was teaching English there and taking courses for her doctorate at Columbia at night. She was very bright and very beautiful, and very ambitious."

"And you were a grad student too?"

"I was a TA in her stat course. I was getting my doctorate too, but I was a few years ahead of her and going full time."

"And?"

"And I was completely smitten, I must confess. I tried, but I couldn't get her out of my mind. I was married at the time, I'm sorry to say. So was Sabena."

He looked down at his coffee cup, then directly at me. "We didn't care. As soon as I finished my degree, I took a job in Virginia and had my wife Kathy served with divorce papers. Sabena completed her coursework at Columbia, left her husband, and came to Virginia to be with me."

"And then you two were married?"

"Yes, and though I'm not proud of what I did to Kathy, what Sabena and I had was what the nineteenth century novelists called 'a grand passion.' It was a once in a lifetime experience."

"But it ended."

Westcott looked right through me for a moment. "Yes, it did," he replied. "I guess they always do."

"What happened? Or is that too personal?"

"No, I don't mind talking about it," he said. "Sabena defended her dissertation while she was chairing the English department at a prep school in Virginia. She wanted administrative work, and there were no suitable schools nearby, so she started applying to schools further and further away."

"And then she moved to Florida?"

"Yes, we thought we could make a weekend marriage work. But we couldn't. We saw less and less of each other. Finally we ended it."

"Amicably, you said."

He sighed. "As amicably as these things get. We both admitted that our work had gotten in the way of our passion and that we were better off unattached. Fortunately, we had no children and few assets to fight over."

"And you last heard from her when?"

"It was right after she moved to Connecticut. She wrote me a short note. I had told her I was moving up here so she had my new address. But we never saw each other again after she went to Florida."

"Not even professionally? At conferences?"

Westcott shook his head. "No, I was traveling in higher education circles. She was in the world of elite private schools. Our paths didn't cross."

"Yes, they are different worlds, aren't they?" I agreed. "Right now I've got a foot in both, and it's a weird kind of experience."

"So I imagine," he said. "Well, I've been completely candid with you. Now tell me a little about yourself."

And I did. I found Richard Westcott completely charming and easy to talk to. He couldn't have murdered Sabena, I kept telling myself.

We spoke for close to another hour, exchanging opinions and information as two people in the same profession will. The literacy conference he was working on sounded interesting but really wasn't relevant to my field. I promised to talk it up to some of my colleagues.

"Well then, I'll look for you at AERA," he said as we parted company.

"Mm-hmm," I replied, but neither of us really meant it. The American Educational Research Association meetings have about fifteen thousand attendees. I thought it unlikely that we would ever meet again.

But I couldn't help noticing how short a drive it was from Newark to Wintonbury. He could easily have driven up to see Sabena and come back in the same night. Of course, that was true of Harvey Konigsberg as well. Had I dismissed Harvey as a possible suspect too soon?

And what should I think about Richard Westcott? He certainly had more energy than Harvey Konigsberg. In fact, I started to think of him as the anti-Harvey. He was almost too charming, wasn't he? Could he have killed her? What possible motive could he have? Could the split with Sabena have been less amicable than he made it seem?

Swash had dinner ready when I arrived home, exhausted from my journey through rush hour traffic.

"I don't know what to think," I confessed to him as I dug into his latest creation, rigatoni with sausage and peapods. "Westcott is a charmer, and Harvey is a sweet guy. And they both loved her, something those of us who worked for her can't understand, but there it is."

"Ah, the heart has its reasons."

"Yes, and neither one of her ex-husbands seems to bear her any grudge. I just can't see either of them killing Sabena."

"Can you see Harvey killing Sheila Lattanzio perhaps?" he asked.

"No, not her either. And really, I think I'm over my Sheila/Sabena fixation now. It was a momentary lapse."

"Does that mean you're going to drop this investigation?"

"No, Swash, I can't. Don't look at me like that. It's not just my curiosity, I swear."

"What then?"

"Swash, there's still John to consider, and I promised Granny...."

"What you mean is that you still care about Wintonbury," he said. "And what happens there. I guess I can understand that. But what now?"

"Well, if we eliminate the two husbands, we're back to Wintonbury faculty and students aren't we?"

"I'm afraid so, but...."

"Ooh Swash, I just thought of something. Do I tell Kathy Marchand how to find Richard Westcott? She did ask me to let her know if I found him. Do I owe her that?"

"Hmm. I don't know about that. If she wants to find him that badly, she can hire an investigator just like Wintonbury did."

"But don't I owe her something? She did get me on the right track."

"Susan, think of it this way: Suppose you're wrong and he did kill Sabena? Putting Kathy Marchand in touch with him is not doing her any favors. Perhaps he is planning on killing off all his ex-wives."

With that unsettling thought, we finished dinner.

CHAPTER THIRTY-ONE

"A practitioner in panegyric, or, to speak more
plainly, a professor of the art of puffing."
Richard Sheridan, *The Critic*

The following Monday was the curriculum committee meeting. When I walked into the classroom where the committee met, my eyes took in the people already there: fifty gray-haired men. Some had beards, some had pony-tails, some were crew-cut and clean-shaven. But they were all men — and me. I knew there was one other woman on the committee, but she hadn't arrived by the time the chair of the committee called us to order.

I felt a tap on my shoulder. It was Dean Simonds, taking a seat next to me.

"Are you going to speak here, after all?" I whispered.

"I'm not planning to," he answered. "I just came to observe."

I looked across the room and caught sight of Scott Jeffries, glaring at me. As soon as he noticed my looking at him, he forced a smile.

The chair dealt with the agenda items in a crisp, efficient manner. When it was Jeffries's turn, he smugly presented the original art department proposal. I raised my hand and waited for the chair to recognize me. Then it was my turn to speak.

"Dr. Jeffries's proposal will not be approved by the state department of education," I began. "Graduates of his art education program will not be allowed to teach in this state. The program does not meet state requirements, chiefly because he has omitted the required education courses."

"Is this true?" asked the chair of the committee.

"Well, we're not so sure about that," replied Jeffries. "We think the state just might approve it. All we know is that we can't get national accreditation with our present program. The proposed program would get us the NAEA accreditation, and then we could go to the state with that and ask special dispensation."

"But that's not necessary," I said. "I have here an amended proposal that meets both state and national requirements."

"I'm afraid Dr. Lombardi is wrong," said Jeffries. "Her proposal does not meet national standards."

"And I'm afraid that Dr. Jeffries is either mistaken or dishonest," I replied. "Here are the national standards, and here is my amended program showing clearly where all those standards are met." I rose and began to distribute the fifty photocopies that Marie had made for me that morning.

"Can she do this?" Jeffries asked the chair.

"Yes, she can," the chair replied. "New information that was not available at the time of the subcommittee meeting may be taken into account at the larger committee meeting. It's in our bylaws."

As the members of the committee read through my counterproposal, I sat in silence. Had I just called Scott Jeffries a liar in front of all his longtime colleagues? Was I still hoping to get tenure at this university?

"Nice work," whispered Dean Simonds in my ear.

"We'll see," I whispered back.

A lengthy discussion followed. I answered relevant questions from professors in the departments of English, mathematics, and history. The representative from the philosophy department made a short speech about standards superimposed on the university from outside governing bodies. Many members of the committee voiced their approval of the philosopher's speech, and the chair began to pound his gavel on the desk.

"Call the question!" shouted Jeffries over the din.

"The question has been called. Let me explain that we are voting now on Dr. Lombardi's amendment to the art department's proposal. All in favor of Dr. Lombardi's amendment, please signify by raising hands."

I watched as twenty-five hands went up.

"All opposed to the proposal?"

Twenty-five hands went up.

"In the event of a tie, the chair of the committee casts the deciding vote," explained the chairman. "I vote in favor, and Dr. Lombardi's amendment passes." He gave a nod in my direction.

"Now the next order of business is to approve the new art department program, as amended. All in favor?"

The same twenty-five hands rose in the air.

"All opposed? Twenty-five, of course. Then once again, I vote to break the tie. The new program has been approved."

"I guess I can leave now," chuckled Dean Simonds, as he rose to go.

"Thanks for the moral support," I replied.

"Next on the agenda is the physics department's request for a change in the major."

I smiled sweetly at Scott Jeffries. He scowled back.

CHAPTER THIRTY-TWO

"If you don't know where you're going, you will
probably end up somewhere else."
Laurence Johnston Peter, *The Peter Principle*

Well, I thought, as I returned to my office after the meeting,
I've won the battle, but I've probably made an enemy for life.

"Don't take it personally," Scott Jeffries had said to me the
week before. I had a feeling that Jeffries would take it very personally. I could only hope that Dean Simonds would be able to
protect me from Jeffries's wrath as I went through the promotion
and tenure process.

As I sat there contemplating my future at Metropolitan, the
phone rang.

"Susan, it's Mark."

"News?"

"Yes! They've found the murder weapon. Caz just let me
know."

"What? Where?" I thought about Sabena's murder for the
first time that day.

"A revolver. Found in Wintonbury Brook. The ice had been
covering it."

"Wow! Anything else?"

"Yes."

"Yes?" I tried to keep the impatience out of my voice.

"Well, if you'd let me talk! Yes, the gun was registered in
Sabena's name."

"Omigosh! Killed with her own gun!"

"Susan, who would know that she had a gun?"

"Well, I had heard a rumor that she kept one in her desk in her office. But it was just a rumor. It fit well with her paranoid workaholic image. You know, working till the wee hours of the morning, all alone, needing to protect herself."

Mark snorted. "Not so paranoid after all. But also not so good a protection."

"So somebody knew it was there and used it to kill her."

"How could someone have gotten it out of her desk?"

"Well, if she wasn't suspecting anything, and she turned around, and they knew exactly where to look...."

"But who would know that? Not some random burglar off the street."

"Unless she heard something, and got the gun out, and then was overpowered and shot."

"No," Mark insisted. "There was no sign of a struggle. It's got to be someone she knew well. And someone she didn't fear."

"Back to the usual suspects, huh?" I thought about Elaine, and how easily she had taken the *Bartlett's* without Sabena's noticing. Could she be that facile at taking a gun out of a drawer? I hadn't mentioned the return of the *Bartlett's* to Mark yet.

"Look, I've got to go," he said. "I'll be home later tonight if you want to give me a call."

"Yeah, thanks, Mark. Maybe I will."

All thoughts of the committee battle with Jeffries were gone. Damn! I'd been worrying about John deHavilland and Sabena's murder for weeks, and running all over creation interviewing people, yet I was still nowhere! Why?

I looked at the pile of lesson plans sitting on my desk, waiting for me to grade them. Hmm. I'd admonished my students to always have a plan, never to try to wing it. But I'd been winging this whole investigation, just doing whatever came into my head.

I needed a plan. A well-constructed, systematic game plan.

And along with the game plan, I needed a team.

It was time to gather the forces together and do some well-coordinated, logical thinking. But who should be on the team? Who could be trusted? Certainly, not Elaine or John or anyone else at Wintonbury. That meant only two people — Mark and Swash.

Together in the same room?

CHAPTER THIRTY-THREE

"I've got a little list—I've got a little list
Of society offenders who might well be underground.
And who never would be missed—
who never would be missed."
Sir William S. Gilbert, *The Mikado*

I left a message on his machine for Mark, inviting him over for the evening, then dialed home.

"Swash, honey," I said. "We're having company for dinner."

"On a school night?" he asked. "It must be something special."

"Yes, it is. I'll explain when I get home. Should we just order Chinese and have it delivered?"

"That's fine with me."

"See you 'round five. Love you."

I closed down my computer, locked my office and headed home, my thoughts in turmoil.

"So who's coming for dinner?" asked Swash, looking up from his computer. Its screen was filled with financial data, and his desk was littered with papers. A typical day.

"Mark Goldin," I said, trying to sound casual.

"The Sabena case?" He lifted an eyebrow skeptically. "Or should I say Sheila Lattanzio?"

"Either. I'm assembling the team tonight for a review of the case. You and Mark are the team."

"And you, of course, are team captain?"

"Of course."

The Chinese food and Mark arrived at the same time. Between bites of moo shu pork and tangerine shrimp, I brought them up to date on Elaine and the *Bartlett's*. Mark repeated his story about Sabena's gun for Swash's benefit.

"Well, you two have certainly been a busy duo," observed Swash. "Aiding and abetting petty thieves and getting inside information from the police."

I cast a guilty glance at Mark, but he seemed occupied with brushing rice out of his beard.

"Now, here's what I want to do tonight," I said hastily. "I want us to make a list of all the suspects. Then I want us all to brainstorm — means, motive, and opportunity."

"Just like they do in detective novels, eh, Susan?" I had hoped that Swash would get into the spirit of this, but now he seemed so cynical. Perhaps getting "the team" together had been a mistake.

"But who do we include in our list of suspects? Everyone at Wintonbury?" Mark, at least, was with me.

"Ah, what the hell," Swash said. "Let's go downstairs and do this right. You give me the names, and we'll make a big chart on the computer. Then we can move things around, add, delete, whatever."

"Great idea!" I was so relieved that he was going to join in, even if he was doing it to humor me. The three of us bounded down the stairs to Swash's office.

Swash stared at the blank screen. "Okay. Four columns? Name, means, motive, opportunity?"

I thought for a moment. "How about a fifth column, for comments?"

"Sure." And now the screen was filled with boxes, just waiting for us to fill them in with our clever hypotheses.

"Okay, I'll go first," I said. "Let's do Elaine. I think this *Bartlett's* thing is pretty suspicious after all."

"A little late for suspicion now that you've helped her return it."

I ignored Swash's comment and went on. "Okay. Elaine. Means — well, the gun. She might have known about the gun, and she certainly is adept at slipping things in and out of her bookbag."

Swash dutifully typed *gun* in the Means column.

"It's going to be gun for everyone then," objected Mark. Swash hit his mouse, and the word *gun* appeared in all the spaces in the Means column. "So where does that get us?"

"Well, add 'light-fingered' to Elaine's box." I said. "That at least distinguishes her from the others. I don't think we can find out who knew about the gun though. The murderer, and anyone else who might feel suspected, could always deny knowing about it."

Swash typed in *light-fingered*. "What about motive?" he asked.

"Sabena was getting rid of Elaine's Shakespeare festival."

"Is that really a motive for murder?" Mark looked dubious.

"The festival is Elaine's *raison d'etre*," I answered. "And I don't know what she would do to save it. Or what she wouldn't do."

"Okay," said Swash, typing in *save festival*. "Opportunity? She lives alone. No one would notice her missing in the middle of the night, right?"

I nodded. "But she doesn't live on campus like some of the others, so she would have to drive to campus and park her car somewhere that wouldn't be noticed. That's a bit risky."

Swash typed in *lives alone* and *car—risky* in the Opportunity column. "I think the *Bartlett's* incident goes in the comment column, don't you?" he asked, looking up.

"It certainly is strange," I agreed. "Especially how much she enjoyed both stealing it and putting it back."

"Mm-hmm." He typed in *Bartlett's* and *enjoyment*. "Doesn't look like a strong suspect to me. But let's see what happens when we get some other people in there."

"Let's do John deHavilland next," Mark suggested. "Means — gun. And if he fled back to his house from Sabena's office, the Wintonbury Brook would be a convenient place to throw it, wouldn't it?"

"Right," said Swash, typing in *brook near home* next to *gun.*

"Okay, then put *loss of house* under Motive," I suggested. "And under Opportunity, put *on campus* and *son asleep.*"

"And don't forget, he threatened Sabena," put in Mark.

Swash typed *threat* in the Comments column.

"And then there's his secret affair with Barbara Gordon. I wonder if that figures in at all. Damn! John is looking more likely than I thought." I looked unhappily at the screen as Swash added *affair* and moved John above Elaine in the list.

"How about Granny Smith?" mused Swash. "At the bottom of the list?"

"Let's see. Means: gun, of course, and likely to know about it with her office so close to Sabena's. Motive: passed over for dean. Opportunity: same as Elaine, lives alone, but would have to drive to the school and park, same problem as Elaine." I watched as Swash entered this next to Granny's name. "Yeah, keep her at the bottom."

"Let's get to some of the others who lived *on* campus, then," suggested Mark. "How about Rob Fleming?"

"Now there's a rotten person. Means: gun and throwing it in the brook as likely as John. Motive: hmm."

"Being fired for all his affairs with students," said Swash. "And he would lose his house, too, if Sabena's plan had gone through. That's two reasons for him to get rid of her."

"Ooh, he's beginning to sound good!" I exclaimed. "And opportunity: lives on campus, can sneak out on Mandy while she sleeps, even though she does provide him with an alibi. I like it. Move him to number one."

"Any comment on Rob?" Swash queried as his fingers swept rapidly over the keys, and the boxes on the screen continued to fill up.

"Yes, he's the only one so far who has an alibi. Doesn't that make him more likely?" I smiled with satisfaction as Swash typed *alibi—set up?* in Rob's comment column.

"How about Harry Trout?" Mark leaned in closer to the computer screen. "Same as Rob for means and motive. He lives on campus and could have dropped the gun in the brook, and he was about to be fired and/or lose his house."

Swash filled in Harry's line as Mark proposed. "Comments?" He looked at me expectantly.

"Bigoted son of a bitch? No, that won't do. Does he have an alibi? Would his wife notice if he were out in the middle of the night?" I was thinking aloud. "She might notice that he had left the bedroom, but since he frequently gets up to drink and spy on his neighbors, she might think nothing of it."

"Okay," said Swash. "How's this? He typed *up at night* and *wife as alibi?* in Harry's Comments column.

"Good," I said. "Move Harry to the number two position. Now, who's left? Oh, Alan Lyons. But what could be his motive?"

"He was having an affair with Sabena, right? Maybe she dumped him and he was angry? No, that doesn't sound right." Mark's voice faded out.

"Well, let's leave motive aside for a moment. He certainly was close to her, so he'd probably know about the gun. Also he could drop it in the brook on the way back to his apartment. So his Means column looks just like John's and Rob's and Harry's, except he had a better chance of knowing about the gun." I hesitated for a moment. "As to opportunity, we know he was in the dorm yelling at the girls around two in the morning. But he could have shot Sabena earlier or later. It would be no problem for him to sneak out of the dorm, except he might meet one of his stray girls on the path!"

"Speaking of which, have we decided that none of the girls are suspects?" Swash asked.

"I just can't believe it of any of them. Unlike the adults in the community, the girls I've spoken to actually sound a little sorry that Sabena's dead. Of course, there are two hundred or so girls I haven't spoken to."

"Speaking of being sorry that she's dead, what about the secretary?" Mark asked.

"I think that Jane truly cared about Sabena. Those were real tears she was crying. And she called the police immediately after she found the body."

"So she said," he replied.

"What about the irate parent you mentioned, Susan?" Swash queried.

"Yes, Mrs. Archer! What about her? Have you heard anything about her from Caz, Mark?"

"Yeah, the police eliminated her from suspicion almost immediately. She was on the road to New York right after seeing Sabena, and has alibis from her husband, daughters, and maid."

"So let's see what we've got," said Swash, wheeling his chair back a bit from the screen to get a better view. "We've got Rob at number one and Harry at number two."

"I like that," I said.

"That leaves John at number three, Elaine at number four, and Granny at number five. And we don't know what to do with Alan."

"Put him in at fourth place and move Elaine and Granny down. It's more likely one of the ones who live on campus. But I keep feeling like we've forgotten someone."

"What about the old dean, McLaren? The one who retired?" Mark asked.

"He's moved to Arizona. Why would he come back to kill Sabena?"

Swash rubbed his chin and continued to peer at the screen. "Hmm," he said. "I know we're all staunch feminists here, but I can't help noticing that the men are all at the top and the women at the bottom. And you won't even consider Jane or the students. Are we being a bit gender-biased here?"

"Well, isn't a gun more of a man's weapon?" I challenged.

"Ahem. It was Sabena's gun, remember?"

"Oops, so it was, but wait! I know who we're forgetting! Swash, you are brilliant! "

CHAPTER THIRTY-FOUR

*"The shrewd guess, the fertile hypothesis, the courageous leap to a tentative conclusion —
these are the most valuable coin of the thinker at work."*
Jerome S. Bruner, *The Process of Education*

"I am?" He gave me one of his most dazzling smiles.

"Of course! We forgot the wives! Harry's wife, Louise, and Alan's wife, Beth."

"Seems to me that Louise would be more likely to kill Harry than she would Sabena," said Swash.

"You're right. And she'd probably use poison in his alcoholic tea. But nonetheless, let's consider her a moment. Sabena was about to fire her husband, taking away Louise's support and that of her two kids. And if Sabena didn't fire Harry, she was still planning to take away the faculty's houses, which would mean Louise's having to give up that beautiful house."

"Okay," said Mark. "We've got motive. Would she know about the gun? If Harry knew about the gun, he might have told her. Right?" He looked at me questioningly.

"Yes, if Harry confides in anyone, it's Louise. Of course, they may never talk to one another, for all we know. So she could walk into Sabena's office, and Sabena wouldn't be afraid of old mousy Louise. And, like everyone who lives on campus, she could have thrown the gun into the brook. But if Harry is such an insomniac, wouldn't he know that she had gone out in the middle of the night?"

"Maybe he would shield her — be her alibi. Maybe he got her to do it in the first place," Swash said. "I think we move her into position number four."

"Above Alan Lyons?"

"Well, you still haven't found a motive for him."

"True. Okay, now let's take Beth Lyons." I stopped and thought a moment. Then I *knew*.

My heart started pounding in my ears. "Swash! Mark! That's it!"

"Huh?" said Swash. Mark just sat there looking puzzled.

"All right," I said. "Let's just go through this whole thing slowly and systematically. Motive?"

"Sabena was sleeping with her husband. Maybe Alan was going to leave her for Sabena. Beth has two young kids." Swash typed in *husband's affair* as he spoke.

"Exactly. Now, means: she might have known about the gun. Alan may have even told her. Like everyone else living on campus, she could have dumped it in the brook." I watched Swash fill in the Means box for Beth. "But it's opportunity that's really key here," I said.

A light went on in Swash's eyes. "Of course!"

"Hey, you two, let me in on this," Mark implored.

"Sure, Mark. Let me ask you, what's Beth's job at the school?"

"Great. We're going to do the Socratic method here, huh, professor?"

"Uh-huh," I said, grinning.

"All right, I'll play. Beth runs one of the dormitories, I think you said. She also has two small children, so she stays mostly in her apartment in the dorm."

"Yes, and that's the way most of the dorms are run. A mother, home with her kids, while the father has a job outside the dorm. I've always thought it wasn't a great job of role-modeling for the girls ...."

"Susan, stick to the subject," directed Swash.

"Huh? Oh yes. Sorry about the soapbox. Okay, so if there's a disturbance in the middle of the night, who would go upstairs and find out what was going on?"

"I guess Beth would," said Mark. "But she didn't. Alan did."

"Now why would Alan, who has to teach at eight in the morning and then spend the day dealing with administrivia in his office, go upstairs at two A.M.?"

"Because Beth wasn't there! I see." Mark stopped to give this some thought.

"Maybe Alan was just being a good husband — letting Beth stay in bed while he handled the situation," said Swash, playing devil's advocate.

"That's possible, I suppose," I conceded. "But if there's major hysteria going on among a bunch of adolescent girls in the middle of the night, don't you think that it might be something better handled by a woman? It might be something about a pregnancy or an abortion or just boyfriend problems. Much better to send the wife — unless, of course, she's not there."

"I think you may be right, Susan, but...." Swash was hesitant.

"Even if you are," Mark said, "the police won't take it as evidence."

"I know. So what can we do? I'm sure I'm right."

We looked helplessly at one another, then sat in silence for a while.

Finally, Swash said, "If we could only lay a trap for her. Is there something about the murder that only the murderer would know, do you think?"

"The police haven't released the information about it being Sabena's gun yet, have they, Mark?" I asked.

"No, they haven't. Do you think there's some way of getting Beth to slip and mention the gun?"

"I don't know, but I do have an idea. It's going to require getting your friend Caz involved though."

"I'm not sure that's a good...." began Mark.

"If I could just meet him and explain...."

"So you've never met this Caz person, Susan?" Swash asked, a smile beginning to light his face.

"No, I...."

"Well, Officer Caz is in for quite an experience, I think," said Swash. "He's about to meet the irresistible force."

It took some explanation and a great deal of wheedling, but I got Caz to cooperate. He turned out to be a young man of considerable intelligence and good humor. And after all, I wasn't asking very much; just to be wired for sound.

CHAPTER THIRTY-FIVE

"If you want anything said, ask a man.
If you want anything done, ask a woman."
Margaret Thatcher, *Saying*

The next day I had to meet with Shauna Thompson and Nini Westmore. I couldn't carry out my plan without the help of the girls in Beth's dorm, and I judged Shauna and Nini to be the most down-to-earth and capable of all the girls I'd met so far. Nini agreed immediately to my plan but the ever-cautious Shauna required a little more persuasion.

I had to get Granny's approval too. As usual, her first reaction was skeptical.

"I don't think we should get the girls involved in this," she said.

"The Wintonbury police have given their okay," I explained. "And really, it's time to get this over with. If I'm right, this will end things, and the school can get back to normal." I knew she wasn't happy about the culprit being a member of the Wintonbury staff.

"I can't allow the girls to be put in any danger."

"Do you think Beth is a danger to the girls right now?"

"No," she replied. "This must have been a one-time thing for her. She's a sweet soul."

"I think you're right about that. She's not a danger. And she doesn't have the gun anymore. So what could she do to endanger the girls?"

"I don't know. I certainly hope we're right about this. All right, as long as the police are nearby, and you're there."

With all arrangements firmly in place, I found the following day of classes almost unbearably long, although the adrenaline coursing through my system certainly made my teaching energetic.

Sitting in my office between classes, I thought about what I had planned. If it worked, we would have a murderer on tape. If it didn't work — well, I didn't want to think about that.

The phone rang, interrupting my thoughts.

"Dr. Lombardi," I said, still thinking about what was going to happen that night.

"Ah, Susan," said the voice on the other end, a voice I had come to dread. "It's Scott."

"Dr. Jeffries," I said through gritted teeth. Perhaps he had called to apologize? Or perhaps to threaten me with reprisal?

"Yes, that's right," he replied in his most cordial manner. "I'm calling to get some advice."

Advice? No apology? No threats?

"Really?" I said. "About what?"

"Well, it's about my granddaughter. She's going into ninth grade next year. She lives in Pennsylvania, and her parents aren't happy with the schools. I wondered if it might be a good idea for her to apply to some boarding schools. And then I thought about you. You used to work at Wintonbury Academy, right?"

"Yes," I managed to say, though my jaw was hanging open in shock.

"Is it a place you'd still recommend?"

"Well, I, uh ...."

"I mean, with that murder scandal going on and all."

"I think that will be finished and the school back to normal soon," I said with more confidence than I felt.

"Yes, of course. Actually, what I meant was that with that scandal going on, I bet it would be easier than usual to get into the school right now. A lot of girls who applied might not want to go there with this murder thing, or their parents might not want them to, anyway."

It would take someone like Scott Jeffries to see Sabena's murder as a golden opportunity for his granddaughter, I thought to myself.

"I suppose you may be right. I ...."

"So if she got in a late application, do you think you could put in a good word with the admissions people?"

He was asking me for a favor. I thought of a dozen indignant replies, but finally answered calmly.

"Sure, I'll see what, if anything, I can do. I'm not sure my opinion carries any weight anymore."

"Nonsense, Susan. They'll listen to you. You are a very persuasive person, after all."

And with that, he hung up.

I sat there for a long while, gazing at the phone. Could anything crazier than that last phone call happen today?

* * *

When evening came, I could hardly eat the eggplant and mushroom pizza that Swash had so lovingly prepared. We watched a movie on cable together, but I was restless, waiting for midnight to come.

At last, after the eleven o'clock news, I started to get ready. I changed into jeans and scrubbed off any trace of makeup. My hair was too short and curly for a ponytail so I brushed it to one side of my face. I couldn't hope to look seventeen again, but perhaps I could blend in with a crowd of seventeen-year-olds. Caz and Mark arrived and wired me up. I put one of Swash's baggy sweaters on over the wires and transmitting device.

"How do I look?" I asked.

"Like a perfect Wintonbury girl," Swash reassured me, with a kiss for good luck. "Are you nervous?"

"A little," I had to admit. "But I'm not in any danger. She can't kill me in front of fifty students. And you and Caz and Mark will be right outside the dorm."

Swash drove me to the Wintonbury campus and let me out on Brook Street. I saw what I assumed to be the police van, parked farther down the street. Climbing Dormitory Hill, I tried to stay near the trees and out of Harry Trout's line of vision. Sure enough, Nini had left the back door to the dormitory unlocked as she had promised. I tiptoed up the back stairs to the third floor commons room, where some of the girls were preparing for what was about to happen that night.

New England prep schools, especially those with a long, proud history like Wintonbury, have customs and traditions that would seem downright bizarre to the outsider. Many of these practices originated with the students in the nineteenth century and have been preserved over the years. Tonight, I was going to be the first faculty member — well, ex-faculty member — to be present at one of these traditions: the Wintonbury Tribunal.

From what I'd heard, Tribunal was a practice used by the juniors and seniors to intimidate the younger girls. A ninth or tenth grader who trespassed on senior turf or was disrespectful to an older girl could be brought to Tribunal, tried, and punished. The faculty and administration heard occasional rumors of Tribunal but had no actual evidence that it occurred. Nini and Shauna had confirmed for me that Tribunal did, indeed, exist, and I had suggested a new use for an old tradition.

About a dozen seniors, including Nini and Mandy, were there, beginning to paint their faces. Starting at the forehead and following a line that bisected their noses, mouths, and chins, they were covering the left side of their faces with black paint. The two African-American girls in the group, following a custom that was perhaps thirty years old (when Wintonbury first began admitting black students), did likewise, using white paint. The effect on all the girls was the same; it rendered them unrecognizable and grotesque.

More and more girls arrived, and the noise level began to rise. Nini had to keep reminding everyone to be quiet. The face-painting continued, and then Shauna, Liza, and Punkin arrived, carrying a pile of black robes "borrowed" from Elaine's costume room.

"What the hell," I said and grabbed a robe. I began to daub my face with black paint.

"Hey, you look just like one of us," Mandy said, smiling in approval.

By one-thirty in the morning, when the ninth and tenth graders arrived, more than thirty girls and I were robed and painted. Twelve of the robed seniors took their places at a long table set up in the front of the room. The rest of us simply sat, huddled close together, on the floor. Nini, as head of tonight's Tribunal, sat in the center of the table, a gavel in her hands. She tapped it lightly on the table. All faces looked up at her attentively.

"Okay, guys," she said, keeping her voice to a stage whisper. "Pretty soon, a bunch of us are going to start making a big fuss, like the night Mandy didn't come back. You can join in or be quiet, whatever. But from now on, no laughing or smiling. This is serious stuff. Okay?" Fifty heads nodded earnestly.

Then Nini turned to the girl next to her and started to whine, "Omigod, what am I going to do? I've got a test and have to get some sleep, and Mandy's not back yet."

Two others took up the cry, "Mandy's missing. What are we gonna do?" Mandy herself chimed right in with a "What are we gonna do?" Three others just kept repeating, "Omigod, omigod!" More and more girls joined the chorus.

"What are we gonna do?" I whined loudly. After all the tiptoeing and shushing, it was a great relief to be able to join in the general pandemonium.

After about five minutes of this, a door was flung open, and Beth Lyons, in a long nightshirt, ran breathlessly into the room.

"What's wrong ...?" she started to say, then gasped at the painted faces before her.

The room quieted immediately.

Nini banged her gavel. "Mrs. Lyons," she said sternly, "you are being brought up before Tribunal. Please be seated." She indicated a chair near the front of the room.

Beth stood among the fifty girls, a look of incredulity on her face.

"Be seated?" she said. "Why should I? You girls are all on notice. Get to bed immediately or I will bring disciplinary charges against you." She attempted to look angry, but I could see that it was mostly fear on her face, which had grown very pale.

Two of the largest seniors moved to block the door. The rest of the girls stood and pressed in closely around Beth. Packed together in the commons room, which was meant to hold twenty girls comfortably, they hemmed her in tighter and tighter. Beth heaved a loud sigh and took the seat offered her.

I stayed back. This was too much like an angry mob for me. And I had set the wheels in motion that led up to it.

CHAPTER THIRTY-SIX

"I am putting old heads on your young shoulders...
and all my pupils are the *creme de la creme*."
Muriel Spark, *The Prime of Miss Jean Brodie*

Nini nodded at Beth, then announced, "We will hear from the prosecutor."

Shauna rose from the floor, her large frame made more formidable by the black robe.

"Mrs. Lyons, you stand accused by Tribunal of neglecting your duty to the dorm," she began.

Beth's mouth opened and then shut. She looked out wonderingly at the sea of painted faces, trying to make eye contact with someone she recognized.

"On the morning of January 24th, we needed you. And you weren't there for us." Not being there for a friend, I knew, was the greatest Wintonbury sin.

"On January 24th, at two A.M., this dorm was in turmoil. One of us was missing. The others were worried sick about her. And when, as we did tonight, we created a disturbance, you didn't come. You sent Mr. Lyons. We want to know why." Shauna's eyes blazed as she got into the spirit of her role.

"January 24th? I... I don't remember. Perhaps I was asleep."

"Weren't you asleep tonight? Why did you come tonight?"

"Well, I thought it sounded like someone was in trouble and...."

"Exactly my point, Mrs. Lyons. Why did you come tonight and not on January 24th?"

Beth looked shaken, but her face lost its pallor. Two angry red spots appeared in her cheeks. "I don't have to submit to this!" she cried, starting to stand up.

The girls in black robes surrounded her tightly. With their painted faces, they were anonymous strangers, not the sweet young girls she knew. They pressed in still closer, and she fell back onto the chair.

"Girls," she pleaded, "stop this. You know I love you and care about each and every one of you. Why should you treat me this way?"

"You don't care about us!" shouted one girl whom I thought I recognized as Tiffany. "All you want to do is bust us when we get drunk!"

"Yeah!" shouted another. "And nag us to keep our rooms clean."

Some of the others made angry noises in agreement.

"Order! Order!" yelled Nini, banging her gavel as hard as she could. "The prosecutor has the floor."

I was glad that Nini had intervened. This was getting out of control. Tears of anger and betrayal were rolling down Beth's cheeks. I began to feel guilty about arranging the Tribunal, but then remembered the higher purpose that had led me to do it. I crossed my fingers, hoping I had been right about Beth. What would I do if I were wrong?

"Now then, Mrs. Lyons," continued Shauna getting back into her authoritarian mode. "Let us go back to the early morning hours of January 24th."

"I don't remember what day that was."

"Then we'll remind you, Mrs. Lyons. It was the day that the Emp — Dr. Lazlo was murdered. Where were you? And why didn't you come when we needed you? Why did you send Mr. Lyons?"

"I don't remember. Maybe I'd been up late with Alix and ...."

"But we *needed* you, Mrs. Lyons! We needed you and not your husband! Why didn't you come?"

"I told you I don't remember. It was so... so long ago." Beth, slumping in the chair, continued to cry openly.

"I submit to the Tribunal that Mrs. Lyons neglected her duty on the morning of January 24th and should be punished accordingly," said Shauna, addressing the girls at the table in what appeared to be a summation. Bless her, she had played the role I'd given her brilliantly.

Then she turned quickly back to Beth. "And I also submit that you neglected your duty for the one reason that would keep you from being here. You weren't in the dorm!"

"But I ...."

Shauna brought her painted face closer to Beth's and glared at her. "You were murdering Dr. Lazlo!"

A collective gasp went through the room. Most of the girls hadn't been told where the Tribunal would lead. Shauna and Nini had kept their secret well.

"I didn't murder Dr. Lazlo!" Beth cried through her tears. "I didn't!"

"Then where were you?" demanded Shauna.

"I went to talk to her. I had to. She was after my... she and Alan were...."

"Yes?"

"But she just laughed at me. She turned her back and ignored me, so...."

"Yes?" said Shauna again. The other students were stone silent, their mouths agape.

"So I took her gun and threatened her. But I didn't mean to shoot her. It was an accident!"

My transmitter and I were sitting about ten feet away from her.

CHAPTER THIRTY-SEVEN

"Eighty percent of success is showing up."
Woody Allen, *Interview*

It was three in the morning by the time Swash and I got back home. Mark had come with us for a little celebration. Caz had taken Beth to the Wintonbury police station and couldn't be there to join us.

"We did it!" I whooped, as Swash popped open a bottle of champagne.

"You did it," amended Swash graciously. "I tried to discourage you, remember?"

"And, Susan, you're the one who kept at it and kept at it, even when we thought we were at a dead end," Mark added.

"Gosh, fellas, thanks. You're very generous, but I couldn't have done it without you, either of you. To *our* success!" I looked happily from one to the other. "And weren't Nini and Shauna amazing to have pulled that off?"

"I couldn't believe, sitting in that van, that I was listening to a couple of seventeen-year- olds," said Mark, shaking his head. "They were remarkable. You must have coached them well."

"I did coach them a bit," I admitted. "But I think Elaine's drama program can take some of the credit. Wait till I tell her!"

"Elaine will be happy to take some of the credit, I'm sure," agreed Swash. "Maybe now she can give up her life of crime."

"And John — won't he be relieved that he's not under suspicion any more?" I said. "Now he can get back to normal."

I thought about John and Barbara Gordon on his front porch. "Or maybe better than normal."

"I think you should send Nini and Shauna big bouquets of roses tomorrow," suggested Swash. "So Beth didn't really mean to kill Sabena?"

"I think she really was just trying to scare her. She knew about the gun and slipped it out of the drawer when Sabena turned her back on her — rudely as usual, I would guess. Sabena was clearly after Alan as husband number three, and Beth thought she could scare her off. Ugh! How could I have felt sorry for Sabena? Poor Beth! The gun just went off accidentally — she was shaking so badly. Then she just panicked and ran away."

"'Poor Beth?' Just last night you were out to catch an evil murderer, and now it's poor Beth?" Swash gave me a sleepy-eyed grin. "First poor Sabena and now poor Beth. Susan, maybe you're not cut out for detective work."

"I think I am a superb detective!" I said, gulping the last of my champagne.

"I think it's time for me to leave," said Mark, hastily downing what remained in his glass.

"Good night, Mark," said Swash, yawning and heading for the bedroom. "It's been great working with you."

"I'll just walk Mark to the door," I said.

"Well, you're a great success, Susan." Mark leaned over to give me a hug.

"I think we have something left to discuss though," I said, taking a step back.

"Oh that, yes." He looked at me sheepishly. "Can we just chalk that up to the heat of the moment?"

"Sure, okay." I hesitated. "But I wouldn't be honest if I didn't admit that I do find you very attractive."

Our eyes met, then he looked away. "Same here," he replied in a husky whisper.

"Well, that said, I suggest we assume our normal relationship from here on. Swash is too important to me to get involved with anyone else, even you."

"Yeah, I realize that now." I could see he was trying valiantly to smile.

"So, drop by my office when you've got time to chat. And I'll certainly call you if another research project comes up."

"Or another case?"

"That too," I said and hugged him good night.

CHAPTER THIRTY-EIGHT

"I believe a little incompatibility is the spice of life,
particularly if he has income and she is pattable."
Ogden Nash, *Versus*

Swash was still wide awake when I came into the bedroom.
"Mark's a great guy," he said.

"Isn't he terrific? I'm so glad you like him too." I snuggled
close. "I can't believe it's all over, Swash. What do you think will
happen to Beth?"

"Still feeling sorry for her, are you? Well, perhaps they'll
reduce the charge to manslaughter, if she convinces them it really
was an accident. What about Alan? Do you think he knew what
Beth had done?"

I thought for a moment. "In some way, he must have known,
don't you think? He certainly knew Beth wasn't there when pandemonium broke out on the third floor. That's why he was up
there trying to deal with Nini and the rest."

"Maybe he just didn't want to think about the implications
of that. Or perhaps he guessed and just decided to shield Beth."
Swash paused. "What do you think will become of him?"

"I guess he's got to leave the school, for his kids' sake as
well as his own. But he's a good administrator. Perhaps he'll find
another school."

"And what about Wintonbury?"

"Ah well, Wintonbury will go on as ever. Once parents realize there's no homicidal maniac running loose, they'll send their
daughters back. And Granny Smith can probably run it just fine

for a while with Jane Ackerman's help. Eventually, they'll start a search for a new headmistress."

"Would you consider applying for the job, Susan?" Swash asked, cuddling closer.

"Me? Good gracious, no. I'm not cut out for that. I'll just stick to my teaching and research."

His sigh of relief was audible.

I settled down into my pillow. "Besides, I've moved on. I'm at Metropolitan now. It's time to buckle down and concentrate on that."

Swash leaned away a little so he could look into my eyes. "So this is Lombardi's last case?" he asked.

"Well, at least until I get tenure."

"Aaaaarrrrggggh!"

I don't think it's appropriate for a husband to swat his wife with a pillow. Especially at four in the morning.

Made in the USA
Charleston, SC
26 February 2015